CHRISTIE JOHNSTONE

A NOVEL

CHARLES READE

1st WORLD
LIBRARY
Literary Society

Christie Johnstone

Charles Reade

© 1st World Library, 2009
PO Box 2211
Fairfield, IA 52556
www.1stworldlibrary.com
First Edition

LCCN: 2009923370

Softcover ISBN: 978-1-4218-8819-4
Hardcover ISBN: 978-1-4218-8918-4
eBook ISBN: 978-1-4218-8720-3

Purchase *"Christie Johnstone"*
as a traditional bound book at:
www.1stWorldLibrary.com/purchase.asp?ISBN=978-1-4218-8819-4

1st World Library is a literary, educational organization
dedicated to:

- Creating a free internet library of downloadable ebooks

- Hosting writing competitions and offering book publishing
  scholarships.

Interested in more 1st World Library books? contact:
literacy@1stworldlibrary.com
Check us out at: www.1stworldlibrary.com

1ˢᵗ World Library Literary Society

Giving Back to the World

"If you want to work on the core problem, it's early school literacy."

- James Barksdale, former CEO of Netscape

"No skill is more crucial to the future of a child, or to a democratic and prosperous society, than literacy."

- Los Angeles Times

"Literacy... means far more than learning how to read and write... The aim is to transmit... knowledge and promote social participation."

- UNESCO

"Literacy is not a luxury, it is a right and a responsibility. If our world is to meet the challenges of the twenty-first century we must harness the energy and creativity of all our citizens."

- President Bill Clinton

"Parents should be encouraged to read to their children, and teachers should be equipped with all available techniques for teaching literacy, so the varying needs and capacities of individual kids can be taken into account."

- Hugh Mackay

I dedicate all that is good in this work to my mother.

—C. R.,

NOTE

THIS story was written three years ago, and one or two topics in it are not treated exactly as they would be if written by the same hand to-day. But if the author had retouched those pages with his colors of 1853, he would (he thinks) have destroyed the only merit they have, viz., that of containing genuine contemporaneous verdicts upon a cant that was flourishing like a peony, and a truth that was struggling for bare life, in the year of truth 1850.

He prefers to deal fairly with the public, and, with this explanation and apology, to lay at its feet a faulty but genuine piece of work.

CHAPTER I

VISCOUNT IPSDEN, aged twenty-five, income eighteen thousand pounds per year, constitution equine, was unhappy! This might surprise some people; but there are certain blessings, the non-possession of which makes more people discontented than their possession renders happy.

Foremost among these are "Wealth and Rank." Were I to add "Beauty" to the list, such men and women as go by fact, not by conjecture, would hardly contradict me.

The fortunate man is he who, born poor, or nobody, works gradually up to wealth and consideration, and, having got them, dies before he finds they were not worth so much trouble.

Lord Ipsden started with nothing to win; and naturally lived for amusement. Now nothing is so sure to cease to please as pleasure—to amuse, as amusement. Unfortunately for himself he could not at this period of his life warm to politics; so, having exhausted his London clique, he rolled through the cities of Europe in his carriage, and cruised its shores in his yacht. But he was not happy!

He was a man of taste, and sipped the arts and other knowledge, as he sauntered Europe round.

But he was not happy.

"What shall I do?" said *l'ennuye'.*

"Distinguish yourself," said one.

"How?"

No immediate answer.

"Take a *prima donna* over," said another.

Well, the man took a *prima donna* over, which scolded its maid from the Alps to Dover in the *lingua Toscana* without the *bocca Romana,* and sang in London without applause; because what goes down at La Scala does not generally go down at Il Teatro della Regina, Haymarket.

So then my lord strolled into Russia; there he drove a pair of horses, one of whom put his head down and did the work; the other pranced and capricoled alongside, all unconscious of the trace. He seemed happier than his working brother; but the biped whose career corresponded with this playful animal's was not happy!

At length an event occurred that promised to play an adagio upon Lord Ipsden 's mind. He fell in love with Lady Barbara Sinclair; and he had no sooner done this than he felt, as we are all apt to do on similar occasions, how wise a thing he had done!

Besides a lovely person, Lady Barbara Sinclair had a character that he saw would make him; and, in fact, Lady Barbara Sinclair was, to an inexperienced eye, the exact opposite of Lord Ipsden.

Her mental impulse was as plethoric as his was languid.

She was as enthusiastic as he was cool.

She took a warm interest in everything. She believed that government is a science, and one that goes with *copia verborum.*

She believed that, in England, government is administered, not by a set of men whose salaries range from eighty to five hundred pounds a year, and whose names are never heard, but by the First Lord of the Treasury, and other great men.

Hence she inferred, that it matters very much to all of us in whose hand is the rudder of that state vessel which goes down the wind of public opinion, without veering a point, let who will be at the helm.

She also cared very much who was the new bishop. Religion —if not religion, theology—would be affected thereby.

She was enthusiastic about poets; imagined their verse to be some sort of clew to their characters, and so on.

She had other theories, which will be indicated by and by; at present it is enough to say that her mind was young, healthy, somewhat original, full of fire and faith, and empty of experience.

Lord Ipsden loved her! it was easy to love her.

First, there was not, in the whole range of her mind and body, one grain of affectation of any sort.

She was always, in point of fact, under the influence of some male mind or other, generally some writer. What young woman is not, more or less, a mirror? But she never imitated or affected; she was always herself, by whomsoever colored.

Then she was beautiful and eloquent; much too high-bred to put a restraint upon her natural manner, she was often more *naive,* and even brusk, than your would-be aristocrats dare to be; but what a charming abruptness hers was!

I do not excel in descriptions, and yet I want to give you some carnal idea of a certain peculiarity and charm this lady possessed; permit me to call a sister art to my aid.

There has lately stepped upon the French stage a charming personage, whose manner is quite free from the affectation that soils nearly all French actresses—Mademoiselle Madeleine Brohan! When you see this young lady play Mademoiselle La Segli'ere, you see high-bred sensibility personified, and you see something like Lady Barbara Sinclair.

She was a connection of Lord Ipsden's, but they had not met for two years, when they encountered each other in Paris just before the commencement of this "Dramatic Story," "Novel" by courtesy.

The month he spent in Paris, near her, was a bright month to Lord Ipsden. A bystander would not have gathered, from his manner, that he was warmly in love with this lady; but, for all that, his lordship was gradually uncoiling himself, and gracefully, quietly basking in the rays of Barbara Sinclair.

He was also just beginning to take an interest in subjects of the day—ministries, flat paintings, controversial novels, Cromwell's spotless integrity, etc.—why not? They interested her.

Suddenly the lady and her family returned to England. Lord Ipsden, who was going to Rome, came to England instead.

She had not been five days in London, before she made her preparations to spend six months in Perthshire.

This brought matters to a climax.

Lord Ipsden proposed in form.

Lady Barbara was surprised; she had not viewed his graceful attentions in that light at all. However, she answered by letter his proposal which had been made by letter.

After a few of those courteous words a lady always bestows on a gentleman who has offered her the highest compliment any man has it in his power to offer any woman, she came to the point in the following characteristic manner:

"The man I marry must have two things, virtues and vices—you have neither. You do nothing, and never will do anything but sketch and hum tunes, and dance and dangle. Forget this folly the day after to-morrow, my dear Ipsden, and, if I may ask a favor of one to whom I refuse that which would not be a kindness, be still good friends with her who will always be

"Your affectionate *Cousin,*

"BARBARA SINCLAIR."

Soon after this effusion she vanished into Perthshire, leaving her cousin stunned by a blow which she thought would be only a scratch to one of his character.

Lord Ipsden relapsed into greater listlessness than before he had cherished these crushed hopes. The world now became really dark and blank to him. He was too languid to go anywhere or do anything; a republican might have compared the settled expression of his handsome, hopeless face with that of most day-laborers of the same age, and moderated his envy of the rich and titled.

At last he became so pale as well as languid that Mr. Saunders interfered.

Saunders was a model valet and factotum; who had been with his master ever since he left Eton, and had made himself necessary to him in their journeys.

The said Saunders was really an invaluable servant, and, with a world of obsequiousness, contrived to have his own way on most occasions. He had, I believe, only one great weakness, that of imagining a beau-ideal of aristocracy and then outdoing it in the person of John Saunders.

Now this Saunders was human, and could not be eight years with this young gentleman and not take some little interest in him. He was flunky, and took a great interest in him, as stepping-stone to his own greatness. So when he saw him turning pale and thin, and reading one letter fifty times, he speculated and inquired what was the matter. He brought the intellect of Mr. Saunders to bear on the question at the following angle:

"Now, if I was a young lord with 20,000 pounds a year, and all the world at my feet, what would make me in this way? Why, the liver! Nothing else.

"And that is what is wrong with him, you may depend."

This conclusion arrived at, Mr. Saunders coolly wrote his

convictions to Dr. Aberford, and desired that gentleman's immediate attention to the case. An hour or two later, he glided into his lord's room, not without some secret trepidation, no trace of which appeared on his face. He pulled a long histrionic countenance. "My lord," said he, in soft, melancholy tones, "your lordship's melancholy state of health gives me great anxiety; and, with many apologies to your lordship, the doctor is sent for, my lord."

"Why, Saunders, you are mad; there is nothing the matter with me."

"I beg your lordship's pardon, your lordship is very ill, and Dr. Aberford sent for."

"You may go, Saunders."

"Yes, my lord. I couldn't help it; I've outstepped my duty, my lord, but I could not stand quiet and see your lordship dying by inches." Here Mr. S. put a cambric handkerchief artistically to his eyes, and glided out, having disarmed censure.

Lord Ipsden fell into a reverie.

"Is my mind or my body disordered? Dr. Aberford!—absurd! —Saunders is getting too pragmatical. The doctor shall prescribe for him instead of me; by Jove, that would serve him right." And my lord faintly chuckled. "No! this is what I am ill of"—and he read the fatal note again. "I do nothing!— cruel, unjust," sighed he. "I could have done, would have done, anything to please her. Do nothing! nobody does anything now—things don't come in your way to be done as they used centuries ago, or we should do them just the same; it is their fault, not ours," argued his lordship, somewhat confusedly; then, leaning his brow upon the sofa, he wished to die. For, at that dark moment life seemed to this fortunate man an aching void; a weary, stale, flat, unprofitable tale; a faded flower; a ball-room after daylight has crept in, and music, motion and beauty are fled away.

"Dr. Aberford, my lord."

This announcement, made by Mr. Saunders, checked his lordship's reverie.

"Insults everybody, does he not, Saunders?"

"Yes, my lord," said Saunders, monotonously.

"Perhaps he will me; that might amuse me," said the other.

A moment later the doctor bowled into the apartment, tugging at his gloves, as he ran.

The contrast between him and our poor rich friend is almost beyond human language.

Here lay on a sofa Ipsden, one of the most distinguished young gentlemen in Europe; a creature incapable, by nature, of a rugged tone or a coarse gesture; a being without the slightest apparent pretension, but refined beyond the wildest dream of dandies. To him, enter Aberford, perspiring and shouting. He was one of those globules of human quicksilver one sees now and then for two seconds; they are, in fact, two globules; their head is one, invariably bald, round, and glittering; the body is another in activity and shape, *totus teres atque rotundus;* and in fifty years they live five centuries. *Horum Rex Aberford*—of these our doctor was the chief. He had hardly torn off one glove, and rolled as far as the third flower from the door on his lordship's carpet, before he shouted:

"This is my patient, lolloping in pursuit of health. Your hand," added he. For he was at the sofa long before his lordship could glide off it.

"Tongue. Pulse is good. Breathe in my face."

"Breathe in your face, sir! how can I do that?" (with an air of mild doubt.)

"By first inhaling, and then exhaling in the direction required, or how can I make acquaintance with your bowels?"

"My bowels?"

"The abdomen, and the greater and lesser intestines. Well, never mind, I can get at them another way; give your heart a slap, so. That's your liver. And that's your diaphragm."

His lordship having found the required spot (some people that I know could not) and slapped it, the Aberford made a circular spring and listened eagerly at his shoulder-blade; the result of this scientific pantomime seemed to be satisfactory, for he exclaimed, not to say bawled:

"Halo! here is a viscount as sound as a roach! Now, young gentleman," added he, "your organs are superb, yet you are really out of sorts; it follows you have the maladies of idle minds, love, perhaps, among the rest; you blush, a diagnostic of that disorder; make your mind easy, cutaneous disorders, such as love, etc., shall never kill a patient of mine with a stomach like yours. So, now to cure you!" And away went the spherical doctor, with his hands behind him, not up and down the room, but slanting and tacking, like a knight on a chess-board. He had not made many steps before, turning his upper globule, without affecting his lower, he hurled back, in a cold business-like tone, the following interrogatory:

"What are your vices?"

"Saunders," inquired the patient, "which are my vices?"

"M'lord, lordship hasn't any vices," replied Saunders, with dull, matter-of-fact solemnity.

"Lady Barbara makes the same complaint," thought Lord Ipsden.

"It seems I have not any vices, Dr. Aberford," said he, demurely.

"That is bad; nothing to get hold of. What interests you, then?"

"I don't remember."

"What amuses you?"

"I forget."

"What! no winning horse to gallop away your rents?"

"No, sir!"

"No opera girl to run her foot and ankle through your purse?"

"No, sir! and I think their ankles are not what they were."

"Stuff! just the same, from their ankles up to their ears, and down again to their morals; it is your eyes that are sunk deeper into your head. Hum! no horses, no vices, no dancers, no yacht; you confound one's notions of nobility, and I ought to know them, for I have to patch them all up a bit just before they go to the deuce."

"But I have, Doctor Aberford."

"What!"

"A yacht! and a clipper she is, too."

"Ah!—(Now I've got him.)"

"In the Bay of Biscay she lay half a point nearer the wind than Lord Heavyjib."

"Oh! bother Lord Heavyjib, and his Bay of Biscay."

"With all my heart, they have often bothered me."

"Send her round to Granton Pier, in the Firth of Forth."

"I will, sir."

"And write down this prescription." And away he walked again, thinking the prescription.

"Saunders," appealed his master.

"Saunders be hanged."

"Sir!" said Saunders, with dignity, "I thank you."

"Don't thank me, thank your own deserts," replied the modern Chesterfield. "Oblige me by writing it yourself, my lord, it is all the bodily exercise you will have had to-day, no doubt."

The young viscount bowed, seated himself at a desk, and wrote from dictation:

"DR. ABERFORD'S PRESCRIPTION.

"Make acquaintance with all the people of low estate who have time to be bothered with you; learn their ways, their minds, and, above all, their troubles."

"Won't all this bore me?" suggested the writer.

"You will see. Relieve one fellow-creature every day, and let Mr. Saunders book the circumstances."

"I shall like this part," said the patient, laying down his pen. "How clever of you to think of such things; may not I do two sometimes?"

"Certainly not; one pill per day. Write, Fish the herring! (that beats deer-stalking.) Run your nose into adventures at sea; live on tenpence, and earn it. Is it down?"

"Yes, it is down, but Saunders would have written it better."

"If he hadn't he ought to be hanged," said the Aberford, inspecting the work. "I'm off, where's my hat? oh, there; where's my money? oh, here. Now look here, follow my prescription, and

You will soon have Mens sana in corpore sano; And not care whether the girls say yes or say no;

neglect it, and—my gloves; oh, in my pocket—you will be *blase'* and *ennuye',* and (an English participle, that means something as bad); God bless you!"

And out he scuttled, glided after by Saunders, for whom he opened and shut the street door.

Never was a greater effect produced by a doctor's visit; patient and physician were made for each other. Dr. Aberford was the specific for Lord Ipsden. He came to him like a shower to a fainting strawberry.

Saunders, on his return, found his lord pacing the apartment.

"Saunders," said he, smartly, "send down to Gravesend and order the yacht to this place—what is it?"

"Granton Pier. Yes, my lord."

"And, Saunders, take clothes, and books, and violins, and telescopes, and things—and me—to Euston Square, in an hour."

"Impossible,' my lord," cried Saunders, in dismay. "And there is no train for hours."

His master replied with a hundred-pound note, and a quiet, but wickedish look; and the prince of gentlemen's gentleman had all the required items with him, in a special train, within the specified time, and away they flashed, northward.

CHAPTER II

IT is said that opposite characters make a union happiest; and perhaps Lord Ipsden, diffident of himself, felt the value to him of a creature so different as Lady Barbara Sinclair; but the lady, for her part, was not so diffident of herself, nor was she in search of her opposite. On the contrary, she was waiting patiently to find just such a man as she was, or fancied herself, a woman.

Accustomed to measure men by their characters alone, and to treat with sublime contempt the accidents of birth and fortune, she had been a little staggered by the assurance of this butterfly that had proposed to settle upon her hand—for life.

In a word, the beautiful writer of the fatal note was honestly romantic, according to the romance of 1848, and of good society; of course she was not affected by hair tumbling back or plastered down forward, and a rolling eye went no further with her than a squinting one.

Her romance was stern, not sickly. She was on the lookout for iron virtues; she had sworn to be wooed with great deeds, or never won; on this subject she had thought much, though not enough to ask herself whether great deeds are always to be got at, however disposed a lover may be.

No matter; she kept herself in reserve for some earnest man, who was not to come flattering and fooling to her, but look another way and do exploits.

She liked Lord Ipsden, her cousin once removed, but despised him for being agreeable, handsome, clever, and nobody.

She was also a little bitten with what she and others called the Middle Ages, in fact with that picture of them which Grub Street, imposing on the simplicity of youth, had got up for sale by arraying painted glass, gilt rags, and fancy, against fact.

With these vague and sketchy notices we are compelled to part, for the present, with Lady Barbara. But it serves her right; she has gone to establish her court in Perthshire, and left her rejected lover on our hands.

Journeys of a few hundred miles are no longer described.

You exchange a dead chair for a living chair, Saunders puts in your hand a new tale like this; you mourn the superstition of booksellers, which still inflicts uncut leaves upon humanity, though tailors do not send home coats with the sleeves stitched up, nor chambermaids put travelers into apple-pie beds as well as damp sheets. You rend and read, and are at Edinburgh, fatigued more or less, but not by the journey.

Lord Ipsden was, therefore, soon installed by the Firth side, full of the Aberford.

The young nobleman not only venerated the doctor's sagacity, but half admired his brusquerie and bustle; things of which he was himself never guilty.

As for the prescription, that was a Delphic Oracle. Worlds could not have tempted him to deviate from a letter in it.

He waited with impatience for the yacht; and, meantime, it struck him that the first part of the prescription could be attacked at once.

It was the afternoon of the day succeeding his arrival. The Fifeshire hills, seen across the Firth from his windows, were beginning to take their charming violet tinge, a light breeze ruffled the blue water into a sparkling smile, the shore was tranquil, and the sea full of noiseless life, with the craft of all sizes gliding and dancing and courtesying on their trackless roads.

The air was tepid, pure and sweet as heaven; this bright afternoon, Nature had grudged nothing that could give fresh life and hope to such dwellers in dust and smoke and vice as were there to look awhile on her clean face and drink her honeyed breath.

This young gentleman was not insensible to the beauty of the scene. He was a little lazy by nature, and made lazier by the misfortune of wealth, but he had sensibilities; he was an artist of great natural talent; had he only been without a penny, how he would have handled the brush! And then he was a mighty sailor; if he had sailed for biscuit a few years, how he would have handled a ship!

As he was, he had the eye of a hawk for Nature's beauties, and the sea always came back to him like a friend after an absence.

This scene, then, curled round his heart a little, and he felt the good physician was wiser than the tribe that go by that name, and strive to build health on the sandy foundation of drugs.

"Saunders! do you know what Dr. Aberford means by the lower classes?"

"Perfectly, my lord."

"Are there any about here?"

"I am sorry to say they are everywhere, my lord."

"Get me some"—*(cigarette).*

Out went Saunders, with his usual graceful *empressement,* but an internal shrug of his shoulders.

He was absent an hour and a half; he then returned with a double expression on his face—pride at his success in diving to the very bottom of society, and contempt of what he had fished up thence.

He approached his lord mysteriously, and said, *sotto voce,* but impressively, "This is low enough, my lord." Then glided back, and ushered in, with polite disdain, two lovelier women than he had ever opened a door to in the whole course of his perfumed existence.

On their heads they wore caps of Dutch or Flemish origin, with a broad lace border, stiffened and arched over the forehead, about three inches high, leaving the brow and cheeks unencumbered.

They had cotton jackets, bright red and yellow, mixed in patterns, confined at the waist by the apron-strings, but bobtailed below the waist; short woolen petticoats, with broad vertical stripes, red and white, most vivid in color;

white worsted stockings, and neat, though high-quartered shoes. Under their jackets they wore a thick spotted cotton handkerchief, about one inch of which was visible round the lower part of the throat. Of their petticoats, the outer one was kilted, or gathered up toward the front, and the second, of the same color, hung in the usual way.

Of these young women, one had an olive complexion, with the red blood mantling under it, and black hair, and glorious black eyebrows.

The other was fair, with a massive but shapely throat, as white as milk; glossy brown hair, the loose threads of which glittered like gold, and a blue eye, which, being contrasted with dark eyebrows and lashes, took the luminous effect peculiar to that rare beauty.

Their short petticoats revealed a neat ankle, and a leg with a noble swell; for Nature, when she is in earnest, builds beauty on the ideas of ancient sculptors and poets, not of modern poetasters, who, with their airy-like sylphs and their smoke-like verses, fight for want of flesh in woman and want of fact in poetry as parallel beauties.

They are, my lads.—*Continuez!*

These women had a grand corporeal trait; they had never known a corset! so they were straight as javelins; they could lift their hands above their heads!—actually! Their supple persons moved as Nature intended; every gesture was ease, grace and freedom.

What with their own radiance, and the snowy cleanliness and brightness of their costume, they came like meteors into the apartment.

Charles Reade

Lord Ipsden, rising gently from his seat, with the same quiet politeness with which he would have received two princes of the blood, said, "How do you do?" and smiled a welcome.

"Fine! hoow's yoursel?" answered the dark lass, whose name was Jean Carnie, and whose voice was not so sweet as her face.

"What'n lord are ye?" continued she; "are you a juke? I wad like fine to hae a crack wi' a juke."

Saunders, who knew himself the cause of this question, replied, *sotto voce,* "His lordship is a viscount."

"I didna ken't," was Jean's remark. "But it has a bonny soond."

"What mair would ye hae?" said the fair beauty, whose name was Christie Johnstone. Then, appealing to his lordship as the likeliest to know, she added, "Nobeelity is jist a soond itsel, I'm tauld."

The viscount, finding himself expected to say something on a topic he had not attended much to, answered dryly: "We must ask the republicans, they are the people that give their minds to such subjects."

"And yon man," asked Jean Carnie, "is he a lord, too?"

"I am his lordship's servant," replied Saunders, gravely, not without a secret misgiving whether fate had been just.

"Na!" replied she, not to be imposed upon, "ye are statelier and prooder than this ane."

"I will explain," said his master. "Saunders knows his value;

a servant like Saunders is rarer than an idle viscount."

"My lord, my lord!" remonstrated Saunders, with a shocked and most disclamatory tone. "Rather!" was his inward reflection.

"Jean," said Christie, "ye hae muckle to laern. Are ye for herrin' the day, vile count?"

"No! are you for this sort of thing?"

At this, Saunders, with a world of *empressement,* offered the Carnie some cake that was on the table.

She took a piece, instantly spat it out into her hand, and with more energy than delicacy flung it into the fire.

"Augh!" cried she, "just a sugar and saut butter thegither; buy nae mair at yon shoep, vile count."

"Try this, out of Nature's shop," laughed their entertainer; and he offered them, himself, some peaches and things.

"Hech! a medi—cine!" said Christie.

"Nature, my lad," said Miss Carnie, making her ivory teeth meet in their first nectarine, "I didna ken whaur ye stoep, but ye beat the other confectioners, that div ye."

The fair lass, who had watched the viscount all this time as demurely as a cat cream, now approached him.

This young woman was the thinker; her voice was also rich, full, and melodious, and her manner very engaging; it was half advancing, half retiring, not easy to resist or to describe.

"Noo," said she, with a very slight blush stealing across her face, "ye maun let me catecheeze ye, wull ye?"

The last two words were said in a way that would have induced a bear to reveal his winter residence.

He smiled assent. Saunders retired to the door, and, excluding every shade of curiosity from his face, took an attitude, half majesty, half obsequiousness.

Christie stood by Lord Ipsden, with one hand on her hip (the knuckles downward), but graceful as Antinous, and began.

"Hoo muckle is the queen greater than y' are?"

His lordship was obliged to reflect.

"Let me see—as is the moon to a wax taper, so is her majesty the queen to you and me, and the rest."

"An' whaur does the Juke* come in?"

* Buceleuch.

"On this particular occasion, the Duke** makes one of us, my pretty maid."

**Wellington

"I see! Are na yeawfu' prood o' being a lorrd?"

"What an idea!"

"His lordship did not go to bed a spinning-jenny, and rise up a lord, like some of them," put in Saunders.

"Saunders," said the peer, doubtfully, "eloquence rather bores people."

"Then I mustn't speak again, my lord," said Saunders, respectfully.

"Noo," said the fair inquisitor, "ye shall tell me how ye came to be lorrds, your faemily?"

"Saunders!"

"Na! ye manna flee to Sandy for a thing, ye are no a bairn, are ye?"

Here was a dilemma, the Saunders prop knocked rudely away, and obliged to think for ourselves.

But Saunders would come to his distressed master's assistance. He furtively conveyed to him a plump book—this was Saunders's manual of faith; the author was Mr. Burke, not Edmund.

Lord Ipsden ran hastily over the page, closed the book, and said, "Here is the story.

"Five hundred years ago—"

"Listen, Jean," said Christie; "we're gaun to get a boeny story. 'Five hundre' years ago,'" added she, with interest and awe.

"Was a great battle," resumed the narrator, in cheerful tones, as one larking with history, "between a king of England and his rebels. He was in the thick of the fight—"

"That's the king, Jean, he was in the thick o't."

Charles Reade

"My ancestor killed a fellow who was sneaking behind him, but the next moment a man-at-arms prepared a thrust at his majesty, who had his hands full with three assailants."

"Eh! that's no fair," said Christie, "as sure as deeth."

"My ancestor dashed forward, and, as the king's sword passed through one of them, he clove another to the waist with a blow."

"Weel done! weel done!"

Lord Ipsden looked at the speaker, her eyes were glittering, and her cheek flushing.

"Good Heavens!" thought he; "she believes it!" So he began to take more pains with his legend.

"But for the spearsman," continued he, "he had nothing but his body; he gave it, it was his duty, and received the death leveled at his sovereign."

"Hech! puir mon." And the glowing eyes began to glisten.

"The battle flowed another way, and God gave victory to the right; but the king came back to look for him, for it was no common service."

"Deed no!"

Here Lord Ipsden began to turn his eye inward, and call up the scene. He lowered his voice.

"They found him lying on his back, looking death in the face.

"The nobles, by the king's side, uncovered as soon as he was found, for they were brave men, too. There was a moment's silence; eyes met eyes, and said, this is a stout soldier's last battle.

"The king could not bid him live."

"Na! lad, King Deeth has ower strong a grrip."

"But he did what kings can do, he gave him two blows with his royal sword."

"Oh, the robber, and him a deeing mon."

"Two words from his royal mouth, and he and we were Barons of Ipsden and Hawthorn Glen from that day to this."

"But the puir dying creature?"

"What poor dying creature?"

"Your forbear, lad."

"I don't know why you call him poor, madam; all the men of that day are dust; they are the gold dust who died with honor.

"He looked round, uneasily, for his son—for he had but one —and when that son knelt, unwounded, by him, he said, 'Goodnight, Baron Ipsden;' and so he died, fire in his eye, a smile on his lip, and honor on his name forever. I meant to tell you a lie, and I've told you the truth."

"Laddie," said Christie, half admiringly, half reproachfully, "ye gar the tear come in my een. Hech! look at yon lassie! how could you think t'eat plums through siccan a bonny story?"

"Hets," answered Jean, who had, in fact, cleared the plate, "I aye listen best when my ain mooth's stappit."

"But see, now," pondered Christie, "twa words fra a king—thir titles are just breeth."

"Of course," was the answer. "All titles are. What is popularity? ask Aristides and Lamartine—the breath of a mob—smells of its source—and is gone before the sun can set on it. Now the royal breath does smell of the Rose and Crown, and stays by us from age to age."

The story had warmed our marble acquaintance. Saunders opened his eyes, and thought, "We shall wake up the House of Lords some evening—*we* shall."

His lordship then added, less warmly, looking at the girls:

"I think I should like to be a fisherman."

So saying, my lord yawned slightly.

To this aspiration the young fishwives deigned no attention, doubting, perhaps, its sincerity; and Christie, with a shade of severity, inquired of him how he came to be a vile count.

"A baron's no' a vile count, I'm sure," said she; "sae tell me how ye came to be a vile count."

"Ah!" said he, "that is by no means a pretty story like the other; you will not like it, I am sure.

"Ay, will I—ay, will I; I'm aye seeking knoewledge."

"Well, it is soon told. One of us sat twenty years on one seat, in the same house, so one day he got up a—viscount."

"Ower muckle pay for ower little wark."

"Now don't say that; I wouldn't do it to be Emperor of Russia."

"Aweel, I hae gotten a heap out o' ye; sae noow I'll gang, since ye are no for herrin'; come away, Jean."

At this their host remonstrated, and inquired why bores are at one's service night and day, and bright people are always in a hurry; he was informed in reply, "Labor is the lot o' man. Div ye no ken that muckle? And abune a' o' women."*

* A local idea, I suspect.—C. R.

"Why, what can two such pretty creatures have to do except to be admired?"

This question coming within the dark beauty's scope, she hastened to reply.

"To sell our herrin'—we hae three hundre' left in the creel."

"What is the price?"

At this question the poetry died out of Christie Johnstone's face, she gave her companion a rapid look, indiscernible by male eye, and answered:

"Three a penny, sirr; they are no plenty the day," added she, in smooth tones that carried conviction.

(Little liar; they were selling six a penny everywhere.)

"Saunders, buy them all, and be ever so long about it; count them, or some nonsense."

"He's daft! he's daft! Oh, ye ken, Jean, an Ennglishman and a lorrd, twa daft things thegither, he could na' miss the road. Coont them, lassie."

"Come away, Sandy, till I count them till ye," said Jean.

Saunders and Jean disappeared.

Business being out of sight, curiosity revived.

"An' what brings ye here from London, if ye please?" recommenced the fair inquisitor.

"You have a good countenance; there is something in your face. I could find it in my heart to tell you, but I should bore you."

"De'el a fear! Bore me, bore me! wheat's thaat, I wonder?"

"What is your name, madam? Mine is Ipsden."

"They ca' me Christie Johnstone."

"Well, Christie Johnstone, I am under the doctor's hands."

"Puir lad. What's the trouble?" (solemnly and tenderly.)

"Ennui!" (rather piteously.)

"Yawn-we? I never heerd tell o't."

"Oh, you lucky girl," burst out he; "but the doctor has undertaken to cure me; in one thing you could assist me, if I am not presuming too far on our short acquaintance. I am to relieve one poor distressed person every day, but I mustn't do two. Is not that a bore?"

"Gie's your hand, gie's your hand. I'm vexed for ca'ing you daft. Hech! what a saft hand ye hae. Jean, I'm saying, come here, feel this."

Jean, who had run in, took the viscount's hand from Christie.

"It never wroucht any," explained Jean. "And he has bonny hair," said Christie, just touching his locks on the other side.

"He's a bonny lad," said Jean, inspecting him scientifically, and pointblank.

"Ay, is he," said the other. "Aweel, there's Jess Rutherford, a widdy, wi' four bairns, ye meicht do waur than ware your siller on her."

"Five pounds to begin?" inquired his lordship.

"Five pund! Are ye made o' siller? Ten schell'n!"

Saunders was rung for, and produced a one-pound note.

"The herrin' is five and saxpence; it's four and saxpence I'm awin ye," said the young fishwife, "and Jess will be a glad woman the neicht."

The settlement was effected, and away went the two friends, saying:

"Good-boye, vile count."

Their host fell into thought.

"When have I talked so much?" asked he of himself.

"Dr. Aberford, you are a wonderful man; I like your lower

classes amazingly."

"Me'fiez vous, Monsieur Ipsden!" should some mentor have said.

As the Devil puts into a beginner's hands ace, queen, five trumps, to give him a taste for whist, so these lower classes have perhaps put forward one of their best cards to lead you into a false estimate of the strength of their hand.

Instead, however, of this, who should return, to disturb the equilibrium of truth, but this Christina Johnstone? She came thoughtfully in, and said:

"I've been taking a thoucht, and this is no what yon gude physeecian meaned; ye are no to fling your chaerity like a bane till a doeg; ye'll gang yoursel to Jess Rutherford; Flucker Johnstone, that's my brother, will convoy ye."

"But how is your brother to know me?"

"How? Because I'll gie him a sair sair hiding, if he lets ye gang by."

Then she returned the one-pound note, a fresh settlement was effected, and she left him. At the door she said: "And I am muckle obleeged to ye for your story and your goodness."

While uttering these words, she half kissed her hand to him, with a lofty and disengaged gesture, such as one might expect from a queen, if queens did not wear stays; and was gone.

When his lordship, a few minutes after, sauntered out for a stroll, the first object he beheld was an exact human square, a handsome boy, with a body swelled out apparently to the size of a man's, with blue flannel, and blue cloth above it, leaning against a wall, with his hands in his pockets—a statuette of *insouciance.*

This marine puff-ball was Flucker Johnstone, aged fourteen.

Stain his sister's face with diluted walnut-juice, as they make the stage gypsy and Red Indian (two animals imagined by actors to be one), and you have Flucker's face.

A slight moral distinction remains, not to be so easily got over.

She was the best girl in the place, and he a baddish boy.

He was, however, as sharp in his way as she was intelligent in hers.

This youthful mariner allowed his lordship to pass him, and take twenty steps, but watched him all the time, and compared him with a description furnished him by his sister.

He then followed, and brought him to, as he called it.

"I daur say it's you I'm to convoy to yon auld faggitt!" said this baddish boy.

On they went, Flucker rolling and pitching and yawing to keep up with the lordly galley, for a fisherman's natural waddle is two miles an hour.

At the very entrance of Newhaven, the new pilot suddenly sung out, "Starboard!"

Starboard it was, and they ascended a filthy "close," or alley they mounted a staircase which was out of doors, and, without knocking, Flucker introduced himself into Jess Rutherford's house.

"Here a gentleman to speak till ye, wife."

CHAPTER III

THE widow was weather-beaten and rough. She sat mending an old net.

"The gentleman's welcome," said she; but there was no gratification in her tone, and but little surprise.

His lordship then explained that, understanding there were worthy people in distress, he was in hopes he might be permitted to assist them, and that she must blame a neighbor of hers if he had broken in upon her too abruptly with this object. He then, with a blush, hinted at ten shillings, which he begged she would consider as merely an installment, until he could learn the precise nature of her embarrassments, and the best way of placing means at her disposal.

The widow heard all this with a lackluster mind.

For many years her life had been unsuccessful labor; if anything had ever come to her, it had always been a misfortune; her incidents had been thorns—her events, daggers.

She could not realize a human angel coming to her relief, and she did not realize it, and she worked away at her net.

At this, Flucker, to whom his lordship's speech appeared

monstrously weak and pointless, drew nigh, and gave the widow, in her ear, his version, namely, his sister's embellished. It was briefly this: That the gentleman was a daft lord from England, who had come with the bank in his breeks, to remove poverty from Scotland, beginning with her. "Sae speak loud aneuch, and ye'll no want siller," was his polite corollary.

His lordship rose, laid a card on a chair, begged her to make use of him, et cetera; he then, recalling the oracular prescription, said, "Do me the favor to apply to me for any little sum you have a use for, and, in return, I will beg of you (if it does not bore you too much) to make me acquainted with any little troubles you may have encountered in the course of your life."

His lordship, receiving no answer, was about to go, after bowing to her, and smiling gracefully upon her.

His hand was on the latch, when Jess Rutherford burst into a passion of tears.

He turned with surprise.

"My *troubles,* laddie," cried she, trembling all over. "The sun wad set, and rise, and set again, ere I could tell ye a' the trouble I hae come through.

"Oh, ye need na vex yourself for an auld wife's tears; tears are a blessin', lad, I shall assure ye. Mony's the time I hae prayed for them, and could na hae them Sit ye doon! sit ye doon! I'll no let ye gang fra my door till I hae thankit ye—but gie me time, gie me time. I canna greet a' the days of the week."

Flucker, *aetat.* 14, opened his eyes, unable to connect ten shillings and tears.

Lord Ipsden sat down, and felt very sorry for her.

And she cried at her ease.

If one touch of nature make the whole world kin, methinks that sweet and wonderful thing, sympathy, is not less powerful. What frozen barriers, what ice of centuries, it can melt in a moment!

His bare mention of her troubles had surprised the widowed woman's heart, and now she looked up and examined his countenance; it was soon done.

A woman, young or old, high or low, can discern and appreciate sensibility in a man's face, at a single glance.

What she saw there was enough. She was sure of sympathy. She recalled her resolve, and the tale of her sorrows burst from her like a flood.

Then the old fishwife told the young aristocrat how she had borne twelve children, and buried six as bairns; how her man was always unlucky; how a mast fell on him, and disabled him a whole season; how they could but just keep the pot boiling by the deep-sea fishing, and he was not allowed to dredge for oysters, because his father was not a Newhaven man. How, when the herring fishing came, to make all right, he never had another man's luck; how his boat's crew would draw empty nets, and a boat alongside him would be gunwale down in the water with the fish. How, at last, one morning, the 20th day of November, his boat came in to Newhaven Pier without him, and when he was inquired for, his crew said, "He had stayed at home, like a lazy loon, and not sailed with them the night before." How she was anxious, and had all the public houses searched. "For he took a drop now and then, nae wonder, and him aye in the weather." Poor thing! when he was alive she used to call him a drunken scoundrel to his face. How, when the tide went down, a mad wife, whose husband had been drowned twenty years ago, pointed out something under the pier that the rest took for sea-weed floating—how it was the hair of her man's head, washed about by the water, and he was there, drowned without a cry or a struggle, by his enormous boots, that kept him in an upright position, though he was dead; there he stood—dead—drowned by slipping from the slippery pier, close to his comrades' hands, in a dark and gusty night; how her daughter married, and was well to do, and assisted her; how she fell into a rapid decline, and died, a picture of health to inexperienced eyes. How she, the mother, saw and knew, and watched the treacherous advance of disease and death; how others said gayly, "Her daughter was better," and she was obliged to say, "Yes." How she had worked, eighteen hours a day, at making nets; how, when she let out her nets to the other men at the herring fishing, they always cheated her, because her man was gone. How she had many times had to choose between begging her meal and going to bed without it, but, thank Heaven! she had always chosen the latter.

She told him of hunger, cold, and anguish. As she spoke they became real things to him; up to that moment they had been things in a story-book. And as she spoke she rocked herself from side to side.

Indeed, she was a woman "acquainted with grief." She might have said, "Here I and sorrow sit. This is my throne, bid kings come and bow to it!"

Her hearer felt this, and therefore this woman, poor, old, and ugly, became sacred in his eye; it was with a strange sort of respect that he tried to console her. He spoke to her in tones gentle and sweet as the south wind on a summer evening.

"Madam," said he, "let me be so happy as to bring you some comfort. The sorrows of the heart I cannot heal; they are for a mightier hand; but a part of your distress appears to have been positive need; that we can at least dispose of, and I entreat you to believe that from this hour want shall never enter that door again. Never! upon my honor!"

The Scotch are icebergs, with volcanoes underneath; thaw the Scotch ice, which is very cold, and you shall get to the Scotch fire, warmer than any sun of Italy or Spain.

His lordship had risen to go. The old wife had seemed absorbed in her own grief; she now dried her tears.

"Bide ye, sirr," said she, "till I thank ye."

So she began to thank him, rather coldly and stiffly.

"He says ye are a lord," said she; "I dinna ken, an' I dinna care; but ye're a gentleman, I daur say, and a kind heart ye hae."

Then she began to warm.

"And ye'll never be a grain the poorer for the siller ye hae gien me; for he that giveth to the poor lendeth to the Lord."

Then she began to glow.

"But it's no your siller; dinna think it—na, lad, na! Oh, fine! I ken there's many a supper for the bairns and me in yon bits metal; but I canna feel your siller as I feel your winsome smile—the drop in your young een—an' the sweet words ye gied me, in the sweet music o' your Soothern tongue, Gude bless ye!" (Where was her ice by this time?) "Gude bless ye! and I bless ye!"

And she did bless him; and what a blessing it was; not a melodious generality, like a stage parent's, or papa's in a damsel's novel. It was like the son of Barak on Zophim.

She blessed him, as one who had the power and the right to bless or curse.

She stood on the high ground of her low estate, and her afflictions—and demanded of their Creator to bless the fellow-creature that had come to her aid and consolation.

This woman had suffered to the limits of endurance; yesterday she had said, "Surely the Almighty does na *see* me a' these years!"

So now she blessed him, and her heart's blood seemed to gush into words.

She blessed him by land and water.

She knew most mortal griefs; for she had felt them.

She warned them away from him one by one.

She knew the joys of life; for she had felt their want.

She summoned them one by one to his side.

"And a fair wind to your ship," cried she, "and the storms aye ten miles to leeward o' her."

Many happy days, "an' weel spent," she wished him.

"His love should love him dearly, or a better take her place."

"Health to his side by day; sleep to his pillow by night."

A thousand good wishes came, like a torrent of fire, from her lips, with a power that eclipsed his dreams of human eloquence; and then, changing in a moment from the thunder of a Pythoness to the tender music of some poetess mother, she ended:

"An' oh, my boenny, boenny lad, may ye be wi' the rich upon the airth a' your days—AND WI' THE PUIR IN THE WARLD TO COME!"

His lordship's tongue refused him the thin phrases of society.

"Farewell for the present," said he, and he went quietly away.

He paced thoughtfully home.

He had drunk a fact with every sentence; and an idea with every fact.

For the knowledge we have never realized is not knowledge to us—only knowledge's shadow.

With the banished duke, he now began to feel, "we are not alone unhappy." This universal world contains other guess sorrows than yours, viscount—*scilicet* than unvarying health, unbroken leisure, and incalculable income.

Then this woman's eloquence! bless me! he had seen folk murmur politely in the Upper House, and drone or hammer away at the Speaker down below, with more heat than warmth.

He had seen nine hundred wild beasts fed with peppered tongue, in a menagerie called *L'Assemble' Nationale.*

His ears had rung often enough, for that matter. This time his heart beat.

He had been in the principal courts of Europe; knew what a handful of gentlefolks call "the World"; had experienced the honeyed words of courtiers, the misty nothings of diplomatists, and the innocent prattle of mighty kings.

But hitherto he seemed to have undergone gibberish and jargon:

Gibberish and jargon—Political!

Gibberish and jargon—Social!

Gibberish and jargon—Theological!

Gibberish and jargon—Positive!

People had been prating—Jess had spoken.

But, it is to be observed, he was under the double effect of eloquence and novelty; and, so situated, we overrate things, you know.

That night he made a provision for this poor woman, in case he should die before next week.

"Who knows?" said he, "she is such an unlucky woman." Then he went to bed, and whether from the widow's blessing, or the air of the place, he slept like a plowboy.

Leaving Richard, Lord Ipsden, to work out the Aberford

problem—to relieve poor people, one or two of whom, like the Rutherford, were grateful, the rest acted it to the life—to receive now and then a visit from Christina Johnstone, who borrowed every mortal book in his house, who sold him fish, invariably cheated him by the indelible force of habit, and then remorsefully undid the bargain, with a peevish entreaty that "he would not be so green, for there was no doing business with him"—to be fastened upon by Flucker, who, with admirable smoothness and cunning, wormed himself into a cabin-boy on board the yacht, and man-at-arms ashore.

To cruise in search of adventures, and meet nothing but disappointments; to acquire a browner tint, a lighter step, and a jacket, our story moves for a while toward humbler personages.

CHAPTER IV

JESS RUTHERFORD, widow of Alexander Johnstone—for Newhaven wives, like great artists, change their conditions without changing their names—was known in the town only as a dour wife, a sour old carline. Whose fault?

Do wooden faces and iron tongues tempt sorrow to put out its snails' horns?

She hardly spoke to any one, or any one to her, but four days after the visit we have described people began to bend looks of sympathy on her, to step out of their way to give her a kindly good-morrow; after a bit, fish and meal used to be placed on her table by one neighbor or another, when she was out, and so on. She was at first behindhand in responding to all this, but by degrees she thawed to those who were thawing to her. Next, Saunders called on her, and showed her a settlement, made for her benefit, on certain lands in Lanarkshire. She was at ease for life.

The Almighty had seen her all these years.

But how came her neighbors to melt?

Because a nobleman had visited her.

Not exactly, dear novel-reader.

This was it.

That same night, by a bright fire lighting up snowy walls, burnished copper, gleaming candlesticks, and a dinner-table floor, sat the mistress of the house, Christie Johnstone, and her brother, Flucker.

She with a book, he with his reflections opposite her.

"Lassie, hae ye ony siller past ye?"

"Ay, lad; an' I mean to keep it!" The baddish boy had registered a vow to the contrary, and proceeded to bleed his flint (for to do Christie justice the process was not very dissimilar). Flucker had a versatile genius for making money; he had made it in forty different ways, by land and sea, tenpence at a time.

"I hae gotten the life o' Jess Rutherford till ye," said he.

"Giest then."

"I'm seeking half a crown for 't," said he.

Now, he knew he should never get half a crown, but he also knew that if he asked a shilling, he should be beaten down to fourpence.

So half a crown was his first bode.

The enemy, with anger at her heart, called up a humorous smile, and saying, "An' ye'll get saxpence," went about some household matter; in reality, to let her proposal rankle in Flucker.

Flucker lighted his pipe slowly, as one who would not do a sister the injustice to notice so trivial a proposition.

He waited fresh overtures.

They did not come.

Christie resumed her book.

Then the baddish boy fixed his eye on the fire, and said softly and thoughtfully to the fire, "Hech, what a heap o' troubles yon woman has come through."

This stroke of art was not lost. Christie looked up from her book; pretended he had spoken to her, gave a fictitious yawn, and renewed the negotiation with the air of one disposed to kill time.

She was dying for the story.

Commerce was twice broken off and renewed by each power in turn.

At last the bargain was struck at fourteen-pence.

Then Flucker came out, the honest merchant.

He had listened intently, with mercantile views.

He had the widow's sorrows all off pat.

He was not a bit affected himself, but by pure memory he remembered where she had been most agitated or overcome.

He gave it Christie, word for word, and even threw in what dramatists call "the business," thus:

"Here ye suld greet—"

"Here ye'll play your hand like a geraffe."

"Geraffe? That's a beast, I'm thinking."

"Na; it's the thing on the hill that makes signals."

"Telegraph, ye fulish goloshen!"

"Oo ay, telegraph! Geraffe 's sunest said for a'."

Thus Jess Rutherford's life came into Christie Johnstone's hands.

She told it to a knot of natives next day; it lost nothing, for she was a woman of feeling, and by intuition an artist of the tongue. She was the best *raconteur* in a place where there are a hundred, male and female, who attempt that art.

The next day she told it again, and then inferior narrators got hold of it, and it soon circulated through the town.

And this was the cause of the sudden sympathy with Jess Rutherford.

As our prigs would say:

"Art had adopted her cause and adorned her tale."

CHAPTER V

THE fishing village of Newhaven is an unique place; it is a colony that retains distinct features; the people seldom intermarry with their Scotch neighbors.

Some say the colony is Dutch, some Danish, some Flemish. The character and cleanliness of their female costume points rather to the latter.

Fish, like horse-flesh, corrupts the mind and manners.

After a certain age, the Newhaven fishwife is always a blackguard, and ugly; but among the younger specimens, who have not traded too much, or come into much contact with larger towns, a charming modesty, or else slyness (such as no man can distinguish from it, so it answers every purpose), is to be found, combined with rare grace and beauty.

It is a race of women that the northern sun peachifies instead of rosewoodizing.

On Sundays the majority sacrifice appearance to fashion; these turn out rainbows of silk, satin and lace. In the week they were all grace, and no stays; now they seem all stays and no grace. They never look so ill as when they change their "costume" for "dress."

The men are smart fishermen, distinguished from the other fishermen of the Firth chiefly by their "dredging song."

This old song is money to them; thus:

Dredging is practically very stiff rowing for ten hours.

Now both the Newhaven men and their rivals are agreed that this song lifts them through more work than untuned fishermen can manage.

I have heard the song, and seen the work done to it; and incline to think it helps the oar, not only by keeping the time true, and the spirit alive, but also by its favorable action on the lungs. It is sung in a peculiar way; the sound is, as it were, expelled from the chest in a sort of musical ejaculations; and the like, we know, was done by the ancient gymnasts; and is done by the French bakers, in lifting their enormous dough, and by our paviors.

The song, in itself, does not contain above seventy stock verses, but these perennial lines are a nucleus, round which the men improvise the topics of the day, giving, I know not for what reason, the preference to such as verge upon indelicacy.

The men and women are musical and narrative; three out of four can sing a song or tell a story, and they omit few opportunities.

Males and females suck whisky like milk, and are quarrelsome in proportion. The men fight (round-handed), the women fleicht or scold, in the form of a teapot—the handle fixed and the spout sawing the air.

Charles Reade

A singular custom prevails here.

The maidens have only one sweetheart apiece!!!

So the whole town is in pairs.

The courting is all done on Saturday night, by the lady's fire. It is hard to keep out of a groove in which all the town is running; and the Johnstone had possessed, as mere property —a lad!

She was so wealthy that few of them could pretend to aspire to her, so she selected for her chattel a young man called Willy Liston; a youth of an unhappy turn—he contributed nothing to hilarity, his face was a kill-joy—nobody liked him; for this female reason Christie distinguished him.

He found a divine supper every Saturday night in her house; he ate, and sighed! Christie fed him, and laughed at him.

Flucker ditto.

As she neither fed nor laughed at any other man, some twenty were bitterly jealous of Willy Liston, and this gave the blighted youth a cheerful moment or two.

But the bright alliance received a check some months before our tale.

Christie was *heluo librorum!* and like others who have that taste, and can only gratify it in the interval of manual exercise, she read very intensely in her hours of study. A book absorbed her. She was like a leech on these occasions, *non missura cutem.* Even Jean Carnie, her co-adjutor or "neebor," as they call it, found it best to keep out of her way till the book was sucked.

One Saturday night Willy Liston's evil star ordained that a gentleman of French origin and Spanish dress, called Gil Blas, should be the Johnstone's companion.

Willy Liston arrived.

Christie, who had bolted the door, told him from the window, civilly enough, but decidedly, "She would excuse his company that night."

"Vara weel," said Willy, and departed.

Next Saturday—no Willy came.

Ditto the next. Willy was waiting the *amende.*

Christie forgot to make it.

One day she was passing the boats, Willy beckoned her mysteriously; he led her to his boat, which was called "The Christie Johnstone"; by the boat's side was a paint pot and brush.

They had not supped together for five Saturdays.

Ergo, Mr. Liston had painted out the first four letters of "Christie," he now proceeded to paint out the fifth, giving her to understand, that, if she allowed the whole name to go, a letter every blank Saturday, her image would be gradually, but effectually, obliterated from the heart Listonian.

My reader has done what Liston did not, anticipate her answer. She recommended him, while his hand was in, to paint out the entire name, and, with white paint and a smaller brush, to substitute some other female appellation. So saying, she tripped off.

Mr. Liston on this was guilty of the following inconsistency; he pressed the paint carefully out of the brush into the pot. Having thus economized his material, he hurled the pot which contained his economy at "the Johnstone," he then adjourned to the "Peacock," and "away at once with love and reason."

Thenceforth, when men asked who was Christie Johnstone's lad, the answer used to be, "She's seeking ane." *Quelle horreur!!*

Newhaven doesn't know everything, but my intelligent reader suspects, and, if confirming his suspicions can reconcile him to our facts, it will soon be done.

But he must come with us to Edinburgh; it's only three miles.

CHAPTER VI

A LITTLE band of painters came into Edinburgh from a professional walk. Three were of Edinburgh—Groove, aged fifty; Jones and Hyacinth, young; the latter long-haired.

With them was a young Englishman, the leader of the expedition, Charles Gatty.

His step was elastic, and his manner wonderfully animated, without loudness.

"A bright day," said he. "The sun forgot where he was, and shone; everything was in favor of art."

"Oh, dear, no," replied old Groove, "not where I was"

"Why, what was the matter?"

"The flies kept buzzing and biting, and sticking in the work. That's the worst of out o' doors!"

"The flies! is that all? Swear the spiders in special constables next time," cried Gatty. "We shall win the day;" and light shone into his hazel eye.

"The world will not always put up with the humbugs of the

brush, who, to imitate Nature, turn their back on her. Paint an out o' door scene indoors! I swear by the sun it's a lie! the one stupid, impudent lie that glitters among the lies of vulgar art, like Satan among Belial, Mammon and all those beggars.

"Now look here; the barren outlines of a scene must be looked at, to be done; hence the sketching system slop-sellers of the Academy! but the million delicacies of light, shade, and color can be trusted to memory, can they?

"It's a lie big enough to shake the earth out of her course; if any part of the work could be trusted to memory or imagination, it happens to be the bare outlines, and they can't. The million subtleties of light and color; learn them by heart, and say them off on canvas! the highest angel in the sky must have his eye upon them, and look devilish sharp, too, or he shan't paint them. I give him Charles Gatty's word for that."

"That's very eloquent, I call it," said Jones.

"Yes," said poor old Groove, "the lad will never make a painter."

"Yes, I shall, Groove; at least I hope so, but it must be a long time first."

"I never knew a painter who could talk and paint both," explained Mr. Groove.

"Very well," said Gatty. "Then I'll say but one word more, and it is this. The artifice of painting is old enough to die; it is time the art was born. Whenever it does come into the world, you will see no more dead corpses of trees, grass and water, robbed of their life, the sunlight, and flung upon canvas in a studio, by the light of a cigar, and a lie—and—"

"How much do you expect for your picture?" interrupted Jones.

"What has that to do with it? With these little swords" (waving his brush), "we'll fight for nature-light, truth light, and sunlight against a world in arms—no, worse, in swaddling clothes."

"With these little swerrds," replied poor old Groove, "we shall cut our own throats if we go against people's prejudices."

The young artist laughed the old daubster a merry defiance, and then separated from the party, for his lodgings were down the street.

He had not left them long, before a most musical voice was heard, crying:

"A caallerr owoo!"

And two young fishwives hove in sight. The boys recognized one of them as Gatty's sweetheart.

"Is he in love with her?" inquired Jones.

Hyacinth the long-haired undertook to reply.

"He loves her better than anything in the world except Art. Love and Art are two beautiful things," whined Hyacinth.

"She, too, is beautiful. I have done her," added he, with a simper.

"In oil?" asked Groove.

"In oil? no, in verse, here;" and he took out a paper.

"Then hadn't we better cut? you might propose reading them," said poor old Groove.

"Have you any oysters?" inquired Jones of the Carnie and the Johnstone, who were now alongside.

"Plenty," answered Jean. "Hae ye ony siller?"

The artists looked at one another, and didn't all speak at once.

"I, madam," said old Groove, insinuatingly, to Christie, "am a friend of Mr. Gatty's; perhaps, on that account, you would *lend* me an oyster or two."

"Na," said Jean, sternly.

"Hyacinth," said Jones, sarcastically, "give them your verses, perhaps that will soften them."

Hyacinth gave his verses, descriptive of herself, to Christie. This youngster was one of those who mind other people's business.

Alienis studiis delectatus contempsit suum.

His destiny was to be a bad painter, so he wanted to be an execrable poet.

All this morning he had been doggreling, when he ought to have been daubing; and now he will have to sup off a colored print, if he sups at all.

Christie read, blushed, and put the verses in her bosom.

"Come awa, Custy," said Jean.

"Hets," said Christie, "gie the puir lads twarree oysters, what the waur will we be?"

So they opened the oysters for them; and Hyacinth the long-haired looked down on the others with sarcastico-benignant superiority. He had conducted a sister art to the aid of his brother brushes.

"The poet's empire, all our hearts allow; But doggrel's power was never known till now."

CHAPTER VII

AT the commencement of the last chapter, Charles Gatty, artist, was going to usher in a new state of things, true art, etc. Wales was to be painted in Wales, not Poland Street.

He and five or six more youngsters were to be in the foremost files of truth, and take the world by storm.

This was at two o'clock; it is now five; whereupon the posture of affairs, the prospects of art, the face of the world, the nature of things, are quite the reverse.

In the artist's room, on the floor, was a small child, whose movements, and they were many, were viewed with huge dissatisfaction by Charles Gatty, Esq. This personage, pencil in hand, sat slouching and morose, looking gloomily at his intractable model.

Things were going on very badly; he had been waiting two hours for an infantine pose as common as dirt, and the little viper would die first.

Out of doors everything was nothing, for the sun was obscured, and to all appearance extinguished forever.

"Ah! Mr. Groove," cried he, to that worthy, who peeped in at that moment; you are right, it is better to plow away upon canvas blindfold, as our grandfathers—no, grandmothers—used, than to kill ourselves toiling after such coy ladies as Nature and Truth."

"Aweel, I dinna ken, sirr," replied Groove, in smooth tones. "I didna like to express my warm approbation of you before the lads, for fear of making them jealous."

"They be— No!"

"I ken what ye wad say, sirr, an it wad hae been a vara just an' sprightly observation. Aweel, between oursels, I look upon ye as a young gentleman of amazing talent and moedesty. Man, ye dinna do yoursel justice; ye should be in th' Academy, at the hede o' 't."

"Mr. Groove, I am a poor fainting pilgrim on the road, where stronger spirits have marched erect before me."

"A faintin' pelgrim! Deil a frights o' ye, ye're a brisk and bonny lad. Ah, sirr, in my juvenile days, we didna fash wi nature, and truth, an the like."

"The like! What is like nature and truth, except themselves?"

"Vara true, sirr; vara true, and sae I doot I will never attain the height o' profeeciency ye hae reached. An' at this vara moment, sir," continued Groove, with delicious solemnity and mystery, "ye see before ye, sir, a man wha is in maist dismal want—o' ten shellen!" (A pause.) "If your superior talent has put ye in possession of that sum, ye would obleege me infinitely by a temporary accommodation, Mr. Gaattie."

"Why did you not come to the point at once?" cried Gatty, bruskly, "instead of humbling me with undeserved praise.

There." Groove held out his hand, but made a wry face when, instead of money, Gatty put a sketch into his hand.

"There," said Gatty, "that is a lie!"

"How can it be a lee?" said the other, with sour inadvertence. "How can it be a lee, when I hae na spoken ?"

"You don't understand me. That sketch is a libel on a poor cow and an unfortunate oak-tree. I did them at the Academy. They had never done me any wrong, poor things; they suffered unjustly. You take them to a shop, swear they are a tree and a cow, and some fool, that never really looked into a cow or a tree, will give you ten shillings for them."

"Are ye sure, lad?"

"I am sure. Mr. Groove, sir, if you can not sell a lie for ten shillings you are not fit to live in this world; where is the lie that will not sell for ten shillings?"

"I shall think the better o' lees all my days; sir, your words are inspeeriting." And away went Groove with the sketch.

Gatty reflected and stopped him.

"On second thoughts, Groove, you must not ask ten shillings; you must ask twenty pounds for that rubbish."

"Twenty pund! What for will I seek twenty pund?"

"Simply because people that would not give you ten shillings for it will offer you eleven pounds for it if you ask twenty pounds."

"The fules," roared Groove. "Twenty pund! hem!" He looked

closer into it. "For a'," said he, "I begin to obsairve it is a work of great merit. I'll seek twenty pund, an' I'll no tak less than fifteen schell'n, at present."

The visit of this routine painter did not cheer our artist.

The small child got a coal and pounded the floor with it like a machine incapable of fatigue. So the wished-for pose seemed more remote than ever.

The day waxed darker instead of lighter; Mr. Gatty's reflections took also a still more somber hue.

"Even Nature spites us," thought he, "because we love her."

"Then cant, tradition, numbers, slang and money are against us; the least of these is singly a match for truth; we shall die of despair or paint cobwebs in Bedlam; and I am faint, weary of a hopeless struggle; and one man's brush is truer than mine, another's is bolder—my hand and eye are not in tune. Ah! no! I shall never, never, never be a painter."

These last words broke audibly from him as his head went down almost to his knees.

A hand was placed on his shoulder as a flake of snow falls on the water. It was Christie Johnstone, radiant, who had glided in unobserved.

"What's wrang wi' ye, my lad?"

"The sun is gone to the Devil, for one thing."

"Hech! hech! ye'll no be long ahint him; div ye no think shame."

"And I want that little brute just to do so, and he'd die first."

"Oh, ye villain, to ca' a bairn a brute; there's but ae brute here, an' it's no you, Jamie, nor me—is it, my lamb?"

She then stepped to the window.

"It's clear to windward; in ten minutes ye'll hae plenty sun. Tak your tools noo." And at the word she knelt on the floor, whipped out a paper of sugar-plums and said to him she had christened "Jamie." "Heb! Here's sweeties till ye." Out went Jamie's arms, as if he had been a machine and she had pulled the right string.

"Ah, that will do," said Gatty, and sketched away.

Unfortunately, Jamie was quickly arrested on the way to immortality by his mother, who came in, saying:

"I maun hae my bairn—he canna be aye wasting his time here."

This sally awakened the satire that ever lies ready in piscatory bosoms.

"Wasting his time! ye're no blate. Oh, ye'll be for taking him to the college to laern pheesick—and teach maenners."

"Ye need na begin on me," said the woman. "I'm no match for Newhaven."

So saying she cut short the dispute by carrying off the gristle of contention.

"Another enemy to art," said Gatty, hurling away his pencil.

The young fishwife inquired if there were any more griefs. What she had heard had not accounted, to her reason, for her companion's depression.

"Are ye sick, laddy?" said she.

"No, Christie, not sick, but quite, quite down in the mouth."

She scanned him thirty seconds.

What had ye till your dinner?"

"I forget."

"A choep, likely?"

"I think it was."

"Or maybe it was a steak?"

"I dare say it was a steak."

"Taste my girdle cake, that I've brought for ye."

She gave him a piece; he ate it rapidly, and looked gratefully at her.

"Noo, div ye no think shame to look me in the face? Ye hae na dined ava." And she wore an injured look.

"Sit ye there; it's ower late for dinner, but ye'll get a cup tea. Doon i' the mooth, nae wonder, when naething gangs doon your—"

In a minute she placed a tea-tray, and ran into the kitchen with a teapot.

The next moment a yell was heard, and she returned laughing, with another teapot.

"The wife had maskit tea till hersel'," said this lawless forager.

Tea and cake on the table—beauty seated by his side—all in less than a minute.

He offered her a piece of cake.

"Na! I am no for any."

"Nor I then," said he.

"Hets! eat, I tell ye."

He replied by putting a bit to her heavenly mouth.

"Ye're awfu' opinionated," said she, with a countenance that said nothing should induce her, and eating it almost contemporaneously.

"Put plenty sugar," added she, referring to the Chinese infusion; "mind, I hae a sweet tooth."

"You have a sweet set," said he, approaching another morsel.

They showed themselves by way of smile, and confirmed the accusation.

"Aha! lad," answered she; "they've been the death o' mony a herrin'!"

"Now, what does that mean in English, Christie?"

"My grinders—(a full stop.)

"Which you approve—(a full stop.)

"Have been fatal—(a full stop.)

"To many fishes!"

Christie prided herself on her English, which she had culled from books.

Then he made her drink from the cup, and was ostentatious in putting his lips to the same part of the brim.

Then she left the table, and inspected all things.

She came to his drawers, opened one, and was horror-struck.

There were coats and trousers, with their limbs interchangeably intertwined, waistcoats, shirts, and cigars, hurled into chaos.

She instantly took the drawer bodily out, brought it, leaned it against the tea-table, pointed silently into it, with an air of majestic reproach, and awaited the result.

"I can find whatever I want," said the unblushing bachelor, "except money."

"Siller does na bide wi' slovens! hae ye often siccan a gale o' wind in your drawer?"

"Every day! Speak English!"

"Aweel! How *do* you *do?* that's Ennglish! I daur say."

"Jolly!" cried he, with his mouth full. Christie was now folding up and neatly arranging his clothes.

"Will you ever, ever be a painter?"

"I am a painter! I could paint the Devil pea-green!"

"Dinna speak o' yon lad, Chairles, it's no canny."

"No! I am going to paint an angel; the prettiest, cleverest girl in Scotland, 'The Snowdrop of the North.'"

And he dashed into his bedroom to find a canvas.

"Hech!" reflected Christie. "Thir Ennglish hae flattering tongues, as sure as Dethe; 'The Snawdrap o' the Norrth!'"

CHAPTER VIII

GATTY'S back was hardly turned when a visitor arrived, and inquired, "Is Mr. Gatty at home?"

"What's your will wi' him?" was the Scottish reply.

"Will you give him this?"

" What est?"

"Are you fond of asking questions?" inquired the man.

"Ay! and fules canna answer them," retorted Christie.

The little document which the man, in retiring, left with Christie Johnstone purported to come from one Victoria, who seemed, at first sight, disposed to show Charles Gatty civilities. "Victoria—to Charles Gatty, greeting! (salutem)." Christie was much struck with this instance of royal affability; she read no further, but began to think, "Victoree! that's the queen hersel. A letter fra the queen to a painter lad! Picters will rise i' the mairket—it will be an order to paint the bairns. I hae brought him luck; I am real pleased." And on Gatty's return, canvas in hand, she whipped the document behind her, and said archly, "I hae something for ye, a tecket fra a leddy, ye'll no want siller fra this day."

Charles Reade

"Indeed!"

"Ay! indeed, fra a great leddy; it's vara gude o' me to gie ye it; heh! tak it."

He did take it, looked stupefied, looked again, sunk into a chair, and glared at it.

"Laddy!" said Christie.

"This is a new step on the downward path," said the poor painter.

"Is it no an orrder to paint the young prence?" said Christie, faintly.

"No!" almost shrieked the victim. "It's a writ! I owe a lot of money.

"Oh, Chairles!"

"See! I borrowed sixty pounds six months ago of a friend, so now I owe eighty!"

"All right!" giggled the unfriendly visitor at the door, whose departure had been more or less fictitious.

Christie, by an impulse, not justifiable, but natural, drew her oyster-knife out, and this time the man really went away.

"Hairtless mon!" cried she, "could he no do his am dirrty work, and no gar me gie the puir lad th' action, and he likeit me sae weel!" and she began to whimper.

"And love you more now," said he; "don't you cry, dear, to add to my vexation."

"Na! I'll no add to your vexation," and she gulped down her tears.

"Besides, I have pictures painted worth two hundred pounds; this is only for eighty. To be sure you can't sell them for two hundred pence when you want. So I shall go to jail, but they won't keep me long.

Then he took a turn, and began to fall into the artistic, or true view of matters, which, indeed, was never long absent from him.

"Look here, Christie," said he, "I am sick of conventional assassins, humbugging models, with dirty beards, that knit their brows, and try to look murder; they never murdered so much as a tom-cat. I always go in for the real thing, and here I shall find it."

"Dinna gang in there, lad, for ony favor."

"Then I shall find the accessories of a picture I have in my head—chains with genuine rust and ancient mouldering stones with the stains of time." His eye brightened at the prospect.

"You among fiefs, and chains, and stanes! Ye'll break my hairt, laddy, ye'll no be easy till you break my hairt." And this time the tears would not be denied.

"I love you for crying; don't cry;" and he fished from the chaotic drawer a cambric handkerchief, with which he dried her tears as they fell.

It is my firm belief she cried nearly twice as much as she really wanted to; she contrived to make the grief hers, the sympathy his. Suddenly she stopped, and said:

"I'm daft; ye'll accept a lane o' the siller fra me, will ye no?"

"No!" said he. "And where could you find eighty pound?"

"Auchty pund," cried she, "it's no auchty pund that will ding Christie Johnstone, laddy. I hae boats and nets worth twa auchtys; and I hae forty pund laid by; and I hae seven hundred pund at London, but that I canna meddle. My feyther lent it the king or the queen, I dinna justly mind; she pays me the interest twice the year. Sac ye ken I could na be sae dirty as seek my siller, when she pays me th' interest. To the very day, ye ken. She's just the only one o' a' my debtors that's hoenest, but never heed, ye'll no gang to jail."

"I'll hold my tongue, and sacrifice my pictures," thought Charles.

"Cheer up!" said Christie, mistaking the nature of his thoughts, "for it did na come fra Victoree hersel'. It wad smell o' the musk, ye ken. Na, it's just a wheen blackguards at London that makes use o' her name to torment puir folk. Wad she pairsecute a puir lad? No likely."

She then asked questions, some of which were embarrassing. One thing he could never succeed in making her understand, how, since it was sixty pounds he borrowed, it could be eighty pounds he owed.

Then once more she promised him her protection, bade him be of good cheer, and left him.

At the door she turned, and said: "Chairles, here's an auld wife seeking ye," and vanished.

These two young people had fallen acquainted at a Newhaven wedding. Christie, belonging to no one, had danced with him all the night, they had walked under the stars to cool themselves, for dancing reels, with heart and soul, is not quadrilling.

Then he had seen his beautiful partner in Edinburgh, and made a sketch of her, which he gave her; and by and by he used to run down to Newhaven, and stroll up and down a certain green lane near the town.

Next, on Sunday evenings, a long walk together, and then it came to visits at his place now and then.

And here. Raphael and Fornarina were inverted, our artist used to work, and Christie tell him stories the while.

And, as her voice curled round his heart, he used to smile and look, and lay inspired touches on his subject.

And she, an artist of the tongue (without knowing herself one), used to make him grave, or gay, or sad, at will, and watch the effect of her art upon his countenance; and a very pretty art it is—the *viva voce* story-teller's—and a rare one among the nations of Europe.

Christie had not learned it in a day; when she began, she used to tell them like the other Newhaven people, with a noble impartiality of detail, wearisome to the hearer.

But latterly she had learned to seize the salient parts of a narrative; her voice had compass, and, like all fine speakers, she traveled over a great many notes in speaking; her low tones were gorgeously rich, her upper tones full and sweet; all this, and her beauty, made the hours she gave him very sweet to our poor artist.

He was wont to bask in her music, and tell her in return how he loved her, and how happy they were both to be as soon as he had acquired a name, for a name was wealth, he told her. And although Christie Johnstone did not let him see how much she took all this to heart and believed it, it was as sweet music to her as her own honeysuckle breath to him.

She improved him.

He dropped cigars, and medical students, and similar abominations.

Christie's cool, fresh breath, as she hung over him while painting, suggested to him that smoking might, peradventure, be a sin against nature as well as against cleanliness.

And he improved her; she learned from art to look into nature (the usual process of mind).

She had noticed too little the flickering gold of the leaves at evening, the purple hills, and the shifting stories and glories of the sky; but now, whatever she saw him try to imitate, she learned to examine. She was a woman, and admired sunset, etc., for this boy's sake, and her whole heart expanded with a new sensation that softened her manner to all the world, and brightened her personal rays.

This charming picture of mutual affection had hitherto been admired only by those who figured in it.

But a visitor had now arrived on purpose to inspect it, etc., attracted by report.

A friend had considerately informed Mrs. Gatty, the artist's mother, and she had instantly started from Newcastle.

This was the old lady Christie discovered on the stairs.

Her sudden appearance took her son's breath away.

No human event was less likely than that she should be there, yet there she was.

After the first surprise and affectionate greetings, a misgiving crossed him, "she must know about the writ"—it was impossible; but our minds are so constituted—when we are guilty, we fear that others know what we know. Now Gatty was particularly anxious she should not know about this writ, for he had incurred the debt by acting against her advice.

Last year he commenced a picture in which was Durham Cathedral; his mother bade him stay quietly at home, and paint the cathedral and its banks from a print, "as any other painter would," observed she.

But this was not the lad's system; he spent five months on the spot, and painted his picture, but he had to borrow sixty pounds to do this; the condition of this loan was, that in six months he should either pay eighty pounds, or finish and hand over a certain half-finished picture.

He did neither; his new subject thrust aside his old one, and he had no money, ergo, his friend, a picture-dealer, who had found artists slippery in money matters, followed him up sharp, as we see.

"There is nothing the matter, I hope, mother. What is it?"

"I'm tired, Charles." He brought her a seat; she sat down.

"I did not come from Newcastle, at my age, for nothing; you have formed an improper acquaintance."

"I, who? Is it Jack Adams?"

"Worse than any Jack Adams!"

"Who can that be? Jenkyns, mother, because he does the same things as Jack, and pretends to be religious."

"It is a female—a fishwife. Oh, my son!"

"Christie Johnstone an improper acquaintance," said he; "why! I was good for nothing till I knew her; she has made me so good, mother; so steady, so industrious; you will never have to find fault with me again."

"Nonsense—a woman that sells fish in the streets!"

"But you have not seen her. She is beautiful, her mind is not in fish; her mind grasps the beautiful and the good—she is a companion for princes! What am I that she wastes a thought or a ray of music on me? Heaven bless her. She reads our best authors, and never forgets a word; and she tells me beautiful stories—sometimes they make me cry, for her voice is a music that goes straight to my heart."

"A woman that does not even wear the clothes of a lady."

"It is the only genuine costume in these islands not beneath a painter's notice."

"Look at me, Charles; at your mother."

"Yes, mother," said he, nervously.

"You must part with her, or kill me."

He started from his seat and began to flutter up and down the room; poor excitable creature. "Part with her!" cried he; "I shall never be a painter if I do; what is to keep my heart warm when the sun is hid, when the birds are silent, when difficulty looks a mountain and success a molehill? What is an artist without love? How is he to bear up against his disappointments from within, his mortification from without? the great ideas he has and cannot grasp, and all the forms of ignorance that sting him, from stupid insensibility down to clever, shallow criticism?"

"Come back to common sense," said the old lady, coldly and grimly.

He looked uneasy. Common sense had often been quoted against him, and common sense had always proved right.

"Come back to common sense. She shall not be your mistress, and she cannot bear your name; you must part some day, because you cannot come together, and now is the best time."

"Not be together? all our lives, all our lives, ay," cried he, rising into enthusiasm, "hundreds of years to come will we two be together before men's eyes—I will be an immortal painter, that the world and time may cherish the features I have loved. I love her, mother," added he, with a tearful tenderness that ought to have reached a woman's heart; then flushing, trembling, and inspired, he burst out, "And I wish I was a sculptor and a poet too, that Christie might live in stone and verse, as well as colors, and all who love an art might say, 'This woman cannot die, Charles Gatty loved her.'"

He looked in her face; he could not believe any creature could be insensible to his love, and persist to rob him of it.

The old woman paused, to let his eloquence evaporate.

The pause chilled him; then gently and slowly, but emphatically, she spoke to him thus:

"Who has kept you on her small means ever since you were ten years and seven months old?"

"You should know, mother, dear mother."

"Answer me, Charles."

"My mother."

"Who has pinched herself, in every earthly thing, to make you an immortal painter, and, above all, a gentleman?"

"My mother."

"Who forgave you the little faults of youth, before you could ask pardon?"

"My mother! Oh, mother, I ask pardon now for all the trouble I ever gave the best, the dearest, the tenderest of mothers."

"Who will go home to Newcastle, a broken-hearted woman, with the one hope gone that has kept her up in poverty and sorrow so many weary years, if this goes on?"

"Nobody, I hope."

"Yes, Charles; your mother."

"Oh, mother; you have been always my best friend."

"And am this day."

"Do not be my worst enemy now. It is for me to obey you; but it is for you to think well before you drive me to despair."

And the poor womanish heart leaned his head on the table, and began to sorrow over his hard fate.

Mrs. Gatty soothed him. "It need not be done all in a moment. It must be done kindly, but firmly. I will give you as much time as you like."

This bait took; the weak love to temporize.

It is doubtful whether he honestly intended to part with Christie Johnstone; but to pacify his mother he promised to begin and gradually untie the knot.

"My mother will go," whispered his deceitful heart, "and, when she is away, perhaps I shall find out that in spite of every effort I cannot resign my treasure."

He gave a sort of half-promise for the sake of peace.

His mother instantly sent to the inn for her boxes.

"There is a room in this same house," said she, "I will take it; I will not hurry you, but until it is done, I stay here, if it is a twelvemonth about."

He turned pale.

"And now hear the good news I have brought you from Newcastle."

Oh! these little iron wills, how is a great artist to fight three hundred and sixty-five days against such an antagonist?

Every day saw a repetition of these dialogues, in which genius made gallant bursts into the air, and strong, hard sense caught him on his descent, and dabbed glue on his gauzy wings.

Old age and youth see life so differently. To youth, it is a story-book, in which we are to command the incidents, and be the bright exceptions to one rule after another.

To age it is an almanac, in which everything will happen just as it has happened so many times.

To youth, it is a path through a sunny meadow.

To age, a hard turnpike:

Whose travelers must be all sweat and dust, when they are not in mud and drenched:

Which wants mending in many places, and is mended with sharp stones.

Gatty would not yield to go down to Newhaven and take a step against his love, but he yielded so far as to remain passive, and see whether this creature was necessary to his existence or not. Mrs. G. scouted the idea. "He was to work, and he would soon forget her." Poor boy! he wanted to work; his debt weighed on him; a week's resolute labor might finish his first picture and satisfy his creditor. The subject was an interior. He set to work, he stuck to work, he glued to work, his body—but his heart?

Ah, my poor fellow, a much slower horse than Gatty will go

by you, ridden as you are by a leaden heart.

Tu nihil invita facies pingesve Minerva.

It would not lower a mechanical dog's efforts, but it must yours.

He was unhappy. He heard only one side for days; that side was recommended by his duty, filial affection, and diffidence of his own good sense.

He was brought to see his proceedings were eccentric, and that it is destruction to be eccentric.

He was made a little ashamed of what he had been proud of.

He was confused and perplexed; he hardly knew what to think or do; he collapsed, and all his spirit was fast leaving him, and then he felt inclined to lean on the first thing he could find, and nothing came to hand but his mother.

Meantime, Christie Johnstone was also thinking of him, but her single anxiety was to find this eighty pounds for him.

It is a Newhaven idea that the female is the natural protector of the male, and this idea was strengthened in her case.

She did not fully comprehend his character and temperament, but she saw, by instinct, that she was to be the protector. Besides, as she was twenty-one, and he only twenty-two, she felt the difference between herself, a woman, and him, a boy, and to leave him to struggle unaided out of his difficulties seemed to her heartless.

Twice she opened her lips to engage the charitable "vile count" in his cause, but shame closed them again; this would be asking a personal favor, and one on so large a scale.

Several days passed thus; she had determined not to visit him without good news.

She then began to be surprised, she heard nothing from him.

And now she felt something that prevented her calling on him.

But Jean Carnie was to be married, and the next day the wedding party were to spend in festivity upon the island of Inch Coombe.

She bade Jean call on him, and, without mentioning her, invite him to this party, from which, he must know, she would not be absent.

Jean Carnie entered his apartment, and at her entrance his mother, who took for granted this was his sweetheart, whispered in his ear that he should now take the first step, and left him.

What passed between Jean Carnie and Charles Gatty is for another chapter.

CHAPTER IX

A YOUNG viscount with income and person cannot lie *perdu* three miles from Edinburgh.

First one discovers him, then another, then twenty, then all the world, as the whole clique is modestly called.

Before, however, Lord Ipsden was caught, he had acquired a browner tint, a more elastic step, and a stouter heart.

The Aberford prescription had done wonders for him.

He caught himself passing one whole day without thinking of Lady Barbara Sinclair.

But even Aberford had misled him; there were no adventures to be found in the Firth of Forth; most of the days there was no wind to speak of; twice it blew great guns, and the men were surprised at his lordship going out, but nobody was in any danger except himself; the fishermen had all slipped into port before matters were serious.

He found the merchantmen that could sail creeping on with three reefs in their mainsail; and the Dutchmen lying to and breasting it, like ducks in a pond, and with no more chance of harm.

Charles Reade

On one of these occasions he did observe a little steam-tug, going about a knot an hour, and rolling like a washing-tub. He ran down to her, and asked if he could assist her; she answered, through the medium of a sooty animal at her helm, that she was (like our universities) "satisfied with her own progress"; she added, being under intoxication, "that, if any danger existed, her scheme was to drown it in the bo-o-owl;" and two days afterward he saw her puffing and panting, and fiercely dragging a gigantic three-decker out into deep water, like an industrious flea pulling his phaeton.

And now it is my office to relate how Mr. Flucker Johnstone comported himself on one occasion.

As the yacht worked alongside Granton Pier, before running out, the said Flucker calmly and scientifically drew his lordship's attention to three points:

The direction of the wind—the force of the wind—and his opinion, as a person experienced in the Firth, that it was going to be worse instead of better; in reply, he received an order to step forward to his place in the cutter—the immediate vicinity of the jib-boom. On this, Mr. Flucker instantly burst into tears.

His lordship, or, as Flucker called him ever since the yacht came down, "the skipper," deeming that the higher appellation, inquired, with some surprise, what was the matter with the boy.

One of the crew, who, by the by, squinted, suggested, "It was a slight illustration of the passion of fear."

Flucker confirmed the theory by gulping out: "We'll never see Newhaven again."

On this the skipper smiled, and ordered him ashore, somewhat peremptorily.

Straightway he began to howl, and, saying, "It was better to be drowned than be the laughing-stock of the place," went forward to his place; on his safe return to port, this young gentleman was very severe on open boats, which, he said "bred womanish notions in hearts naturally dauntless. Give me a lid to the pot," added he, "and I'll sail with Old Nick, let the wind blow high or low."

The Aberford was wrong when he called love a cutaneous disorder.

There are cutaneous disorders that take that name, but they are no more love than verse is poetry;

Than patriotism is love of country;

Than theology is religion;

Than science is philosophy;

Than paintings are pictures;

Than reciting on the boards is acting;

Than physic is medicine

Than bread is bread, or gold gold—in shops.

Love is a state of being; the beloved object is our center; and our thoughts, affections, schemes and selves move but round it.

We may diverge hither or thither, but the golden thread still

Charles Reade

holds us.

Is fair or dark beauty the fairest? The world cannot decide; but love shall decide in a moment.

A halo surrounds her we love, and makes beautiful to us her movements, her looks, her virtues, her faults, her nonsense, her affectation and herself; and that's love, doctor!

Lord Ipsden was capable of loving like this; but, to do Lady Barbara justice, she had done much to freeze the germ of noble passion; she had not killed, but she had benumbed it.

"Saunders," said Lord Ipsden, one morning after breakfast, "have you entered everything in your diary?"

"Yes, my lord."

"All these good people's misfortunes?"

"Yes, my lord."

"Do you think you have spelled their names right?"

"Where it was impossible, my lord, I substituted an English appellation, hidentical in meaning."

"Have you entered and described my first interview with Christie Johnstone, and somebody something?"

"Most minutely, my lord."

"How I turned Mr. Burke into poetry—how she listened with her eyes all glistening—how they made me talk—how she dropped a tear, he! he! he! at the death of the first baron—how shocked she was at the king striking him when he was dying, to make a knight-banneret of the poor old fellow?"

"Your lordship will find all the particulars exactly related," said Saunders, with dry pomp.

"How she found out that titles are but breath—how I answered—some nonsense?"

"Your lordship will find all the topics included."

"How she took me for a madman? And you for a prig?"

"The latter circumstance eluded my memory, my lord."

"But when I told her I must relieve only one poor person by day, she took my hand."

"Your lordship will find all the items realized in this book, my lord."

"What a beautiful book!"

"Alba are considerably ameliorated, my lord."

"Alba?"

"Plural of album, my lord," explained the refined factotum, "more delicate, I conceive, than the vulgar reading."

Viscount Ipsden read from

"MR. SAUNDERS'S ALBUM.

"To illustrate the inelegance of the inferior classes, two juvenile venders of the piscatory tribe were this day ushered in, and instantaneously, without the accustomed preliminaries, plunged into a familiar conversation with Lord Viscount Ipsden.

"Their vulgarity, shocking and repulsive to myself, appeared to afford his lordship a satisfaction greater than he derives from the graceful amenities of fashionable association—"

"Saunders, I suspect you of something."

"Me, my lord!"

"Yes. Writing in an annual."

"I do, my lord," said he, with benignant *hauteur.* "It appears every month—*The Polytechnic.*"

"I thought so! you are polysyllabic, Saunders; *en route!*"

"In this hallucination I find it difficult to participate; associated from infancy with the aristocracy, I shrink, like the sensitive plant, from contact with anything vulgar."

"I see! I begin to understand you, Saunders. Order the dog-cart, and Wordsworth's mare for leader; we'll give her a trial. You are an ass, Saunders."

"Yes, my lord; I will order Robert to tell James to come for your lordship's commands about your lordship's vehicles. (What could he intend by a recent observation of a discourteous character?)"

His lordship soliloquized.

"I never observed it before, but Saunders is an ass! La Johnstone is one of Nature's duchesses, and she has made me know some poor people that will be richer than the rich one day; and she has taught me that honey is to be got from bank-notes—by merely giving them away."

Among the objects of charity Lord Ipsden discovered was one Thomas Harvey, a maker and player of the violin. This man was a person of great intellect; he mastered every subject he attacked. By a careful examination of all the points that various fine-toned instruments had in common, he had arrived at a theory of sound; he made violins to correspond, and was remarkably successful in insuring that which had been too hastily ascribed to accident—a fine tone.

This man, who was in needy circumstances, demonstrated to his lordship that ten pounds would make his fortune; because with ten pounds he could set up a shop, instead of working out of the world's sight in a room.

Lord Ipsden gave him ten pounds!

A week after, he met Harvey, more ragged and dirty than before.

Harvey had been robbed by a friend whom he had assisted. Poor Harvey! Lord Ipsden gave him ten pounds more!

Next week, Saunders, entering Harvey's house, found him in bed at noon, because he had no clothes to wear.

Saunders suggested that it would be better to give his wife the next money, with strict orders to apply it usefully.

This was done!

The next day, Harvey, finding his clothes upon a chair, his tools redeemed from pawn, and a beefsteak ready for his dinner, accused his wife of having money, and meanly refusing him the benefit of it. She acknowledged she had a little, and appealed to the improved state of things as a proof that she knew better than he the use of money. He demanded the said money. She refused—he leathered her—she put him in prison.

This was the best place for him. The man was a drunkard, and all the riches of Egypt would never have made him better off.

And here, gentlemen of the lower classes, a word with you. How can you, with your small incomes, hope to be well off, if you are more extravagant than those who have large ones?

"Us extravagant?" you reply.

Yes! your income is ten shillings a week; out of that you spend three shillings in drink; ay! you, the sober ones. You can't afford it, my boys. Find me a man whose income is a thousand a year; well, if he imitates you, and spends three hundred upon sensuality, I bet you the odd seven hundred he does not make both ends meet; the proportion is too great. And *two-thirds of the distress of the lower orders is owing to this—that they are more madly prodigal than the rich; in the worst, lowest and most dangerous item of all human prodigality!*

Lord Ipsden went to see Mrs. Harvey; it cost him much to go; she lived in the Old Town, and he hated disagreeable smells; he also knew from Saunders that she had two black eyes, and he hated women with black eyes of that sort. But this good creature did go; did relieve Mrs. Harvey; and, bare-headed, suffered himself to be bedewed ten minutes by her tearful twaddle.

For once Virtue was rewarded. Returning over the North Bridge, he met somebody whom but for his charity he would not have met.

He came in one bright moment plump upon—Lady Barbara Sinclair. She flushed, he trembled, and in two minutes he had forgotten every human event that had passed since he was by her side.

She seemed pleased to see him, too; she ignored entirely his obnoxious proposal; he wisely took her cue, and so, on this secret understanding, they were friends. He made his arrangements, and dined with her family. It was a family party. In the evening Lady Barbara allowed it to transpire that she had made inquiries about him.

(He was highly flattered.) And she had discovered he was lying hid somewhere in the neighborhood.

"Studying the guitar?" inquired she.

"No," said he, "studying a new class of the community. Do you know any of what they call the 'lower classes'?"

"Yes."

"Monstrous agreeable people, are they not?"

"No, very stupid! I only know two old women—except the servants, who have no characters. They imitate us, I suspect, which does not say much for their taste."

"But some of my friends are young women; that makes all the difference."

"It does! and you ought to be ashamed. If you want a low order of mind, why desert our own circle?"

"My friends are only low in station; they have rather lofty minds, some of them."

"Well, amuse yourself with these lofty minds. Amusement is the end of being, you know, and the aim of all the men of this day."

"We imitate the ladies," said he, slyly.

"You do," answered she, very dryly; and so the dialogue went on, and Lord Ipsden found the pleasure of being with his cousin compensate him fully for the difference of their opinions; in fact, he found it simply amusing that so keen a wit as his cousins s could be entrapped into the humor of decrying the time one happens to live in, and admiring any epoch one knows next to nothing about, and entrapped by the notion of its originality, above all things; the idea being the stale commonplace of asses in every age, and the manner of conveying the idea being a mere imitation of the German writers, not the good ones, *bien entendu,* but the quill-drivers, the snobs of the Teutonic pen.

But he was to learn that follies are not always laughable, that *eadem sentire* is a bond, and that, when a clever and pretty woman chooses to be a fool, her lover, if he is wise, will be a greater—if he can.

The next time they met, Lord Ipsden found Lady Barbara occupied with a gentleman whose first sentence proclaimed him a pupil of Mr. Thomas Carlyle, and he had the mortification to find that she had neither an ear nor an eye for him.

Human opinion has so many shades that it is rare to find two people agree.

But two people may agree wonderfully, if they will but let a third think for them both.

Thus it was that these two ran so smoothly in couples.

Antiquity, they agreed, was the time when the world was old, its hair gray, its head wise. Every one that said, "Lord, Lord!" two hundred years ago was a Christian. There were no earnest men now; Williams, the missionary, who lived and died for the Gospel, was not earnest in religion; but Cromwell, who packed a jury, and so murdered his prisoner—Cromwell, in whose mouth was heaven, and in his heart temporal sovereignty—was the pattern of earnest religion, or, at all events, second in sincerity to Mahomet alone, in the absence of details respecting Satan, of whom we know only that his mouth is a Scripture concordance, and his hands the hands of Mr. Carlyle's saints.

Then they went back a century or two, and were eloquent about the great antique heart, and the beauty of an age whose samples were Abbot Sampson and Joan of Arc.

Lord Ipsden hated argument; but jealousy is a brass spur, it made even this man fluent for once.

He suggested "that five hundred years added to a world's life made it just five hundred years older, not younger—and if older, grayer—and if grayer, wiser.

"Of Abbot Sampson," said he, "whom I confess both a great and a good man, his author, who with all his talent belongs to the class muddle-head, tells us that when he had been two years in authority his red hair had turned gray, fighting against the spirit of his age; how the deuce, then, could he be a sample of the spirit of his age?

"Joan of Arc was burned by acclamation of her age, and is admired by our age. Which fact identifies an age most with a heroine, to give her your heart, or to give her a blazing fagot and death?"

"Abbot Sampson and Joan of Arc," concluded he, "prove no more in favor of their age, and no less against it, than Lot does for or against Sodom. Lot was in Sodom, but not of it; and so were Sampson and Joan in, but not of, the villainous times they lived in.

"The very best text-book of true religion is the New Testament, and I gather from it, that the man who forgives his enemies while their ax descends on his head, however poor a creature he may be in other respects, is a better Christian than the man who has the God of Mercy forever on his lips, and whose hands are swift to shed blood.

"The earnest men of former ages are not extinct in this," added he. "Whenever a scaffold is erected outside a prison-door, if you are earnest in pursuit of truth, and can put up with disgusting objects, you shall see a relic of ancient manners hanged.

"There still exist, in parts of America, rivers on whose banks are earnest men who shall take your scalp, the wife's of your bosom, and the innocent child's of her bosom.

"In England we are as earnest as ever in pursuit of heaven, and of innocent worldly advantages. If, when the consideration of life and death interposes, we appear less earnest in pursuit of comparative trifles such as kingdoms or dogmas, it is because cooler in action we are more earnest in thought—because reason, experience, and conscience are things that check the unscrupulousness or beastly earnestness of man.

"Moreover, he who has the sense to see that questions have three sides is no longer so intellectually as well as morally degraded as to be able to cut every throat that utters an opinion contrary to his own.

"If the phrase 'earnest man' means man imitating the beasts that are deaf to reason, it is to be hoped that civilization and Christianity will really extinguish the whole race for the benefit of the earth."

Lord Ipsden succeeded in annoying the fair theorist, but not in convincing her.

The mediaeval enthusiasts looked on him as some rough animal that had burst into sacred grounds unconsciously, and gradually edged away from him.

CHAPTER X

LORD IPSDEN had soon the mortification of discovering that this Mr.—was a constant visitor at the house; and, although his cousin gave him her ear in this man's absence, on the arrival of her fellow-enthusiast he had ever the mortification of finding himself *de trop.*

Once or twice he demolished this personage in argument, and was rewarded by finding himself more *de trop.*

But one day Lady Barbara, being in a cousinly humor, expressed a wish to sail in his lordship's yacht, and this hint soon led to a party being organized, and a sort of picnic on the island of Inch Coombe; his lordship's cutter being the mode of conveyance to and from that spot.

Now it happened on that very day Jean Carnie's marriage was celebrated on that very island by her relations and friends.

So that we shall introduce our readers to

THE RIVAL PICNICS.

We begin with *Les gens comme il faut.*

PICNIC NO. 1.

The servants were employed in putting away dishes into hampers.

There was a calm silence. "Hem!" observed Sir Henry Talbot.

"Eh?" replied the Honorable Tom Hitherington.

"Mamma," said Miss Vere, "have you brought any work?"

"No, my dear."

"At a picnic," said Mr. Hitherington, isn't it the thing for somebody—aw—to do something?"

"Ipsden," said Lady Barbara, "there is an understanding *between* you and Mr. Hitherington. I condemn you to turn him into English."

"Yes, Lady Barbara; I'll tell you, he means—-do you mean anything, Tom?"

Hitherington. "Can't anybody guess what I mean?"

Lady Barbara. "Guess first yourself, you can't be suspected of being in the secret."

Hither. "What I mean is, that people sing a song, or run races, or preach a sermon, or do something funny at a picnic —aw—somebody gets up and does something."

Lady Bar. "Then perhaps Miss Vere, whose singing is famous, will have the complaisance to sing to us."

Charles Reade

Miss Vere. "I should be happy, Lady Barbara, but I have not brought my music."

Lady Bar. "Oh, we are not critical; the simplest air, or even a fragment of melody; the sea and the sky will be a better accompaniment than Broadwood ever made."

Miss V. "I can't sing a note without book."

Sir H. Talbot. "Your music is in your soul—not at your fingers' ends."

Lord Ipsden, to Lady Bar. "It is in her book, and not in her soul."

Lady Bar., to Lord Ips. "Then it has chosen the better situation of the two."

Ips. "Miss Vere is to the fine art of music what the engrossers are to the black art of law; it all filters through them without leaving any sediment; and so the music of the day passes through Miss Vere's mind, but none remains—to stain its virgin snow."

He bows, she smiles.

Lady Bar., to herself. "Insolent. And the little dunce thinks he is complimenting her."

Ips. "Perhaps Talbot will come to our rescue—he is a fiddler."

Tal. "An amateur of the violin."

Ips. "It is all the same thing."

Lady Bar. "I wish it may prove so."

[Note: original has music notation here]

Miss V. "Beautiful."

Mrs. Vere. "Charming."

Hither. "Superb!"

Ips. "You are aware that good music is a thing to be wedded to immortal verse, shall I recite a bit of poetry to match Talbot's strain?"

Miss V. "Oh, yes! how nice."

Ips. (rhetorically). "A. B. C. D. E. F. G. H. I. J. K. L. M. N. O. P. Q. R. S. T. U. V. W. X. Y. Z. Y. X. W. V. U. T. S. O. N. M. L. K. J. I. H. G. F. A. M. little p. little t."

Lady Bar. "Beautiful! Superb! Ipsden has been taking lessons on the thinking instrument."

Hither. "He has been *perdu* among vulgar people."

Tal. "And expects a pupil of Herz to play him tunes!"

Lady Bar. "What are tunes, Sir Henry?"

Tal. "Something I don't play, Lady Barbara."

Lady Bar. "I understand you; something we ought to like."

Ips. "I have a Stradivarius violin at home. It is yours, Talbot, if you can define a tune."

Charles Reade

Tal. "A tune is—everybody knows what."

Lady Bar. "A tune is a tune, that is what you meant to say."

Tal. "Of course it is."

Lady Bar. "Be reasonable, Ipsden; no man can do two things at once; how can the pupil of Herz condemn a thing and know what it means contemporaneously?"

Ips. "Is the drinking-song in 'Der Freischutz' a tune?"

Lady Bar. "It is."

Ips. "And the melodies of Handel, are they tunes?"

Lady Bar. (pathetically). "They are! They are!"

Ips. "And the 'Russian Anthem,' and the 'Marseillaise,' and 'Ah, Perdona'?"

Tal. "And 'Yankee Doodle'?"

Lady Bar. "So that Sir Henry, who prided himself on his ignorance, has a wide field for its dominion.

Tal. "All good violin players do like me; they prelude, not play tunes."

Ips. "Then Heaven be thanked for our blind fiddlers. You like syllables of sound in unmeaning rotation, and you despise its words, its purposes, its narrative feats; carry out your principle, it will show you where you are. Buy a dirty palette for a picture, and dream the alphabet is a poem."

Lady Bar., to herself. "Is this my cousin Richard?"

Hither. "Mind, Ipsden, you are a man of property, and there are such things as commissions *de lunatico.*"

Lady Bar. "His defense will be that his friends pronounced him insane.

Ips. "No; I shall subpoena Talbot's fiddle, cross-examination will get nothing out of that but, do, re, mi, fa."

Lady Bar. "Yes, it will; fa, mi, re, do."

Tal. "Violin, if you please."

Lady Bar. "Ask Fiddle's pardon, directly."

Sound of fiddles is heard in the distance.

Tal. "How lucky for you, there are fiddles and tunes, and the natives you are said to favor, why not join them?"

Ips. (shaking his head solemnly). "I dread to encounter another prelude."

Hither. "Come, I know you would like it; it is a wedding-party—two sea monsters have been united. The sailors and fishermen are all blue cloth and wash-leather gloves."

Miss V. "He! he!"

Tal. "The fishwives unite the colors of the rainbow—"

Lady Bar. "(And we all know how hideous they are)—to vulgar, blooming cheeks, staring white teeth, and sky-blue eyes."

Mrs. V. "How satirical you are, especially you, Lady Barbara."

Here Lord Ipsden, after a word to Lady Barbara, the answer to which did not appear to be favorable, rose, gave a little yawn, looked steadily at his companions without seeing them, and departed without seeming aware that he was leaving anybody behind him.

Hither. "Let us go somewhere where we can quiz the natives without being too near them."

Lady Bar. "I am tired of this unbroken solitude, I must go and think to the sea," added she, in a mock soliloquy; and out she glided with the same unconscious air as his lordship had worn.

The others moved off slowly together.

"Mamma," said Miss Vere," I can't understand half Barbara Sinclair says."

"It is not necessary, my love," replied mamma; "she is rather eccentric, and I fear she is spoiling Lord Ipsden."

"Poor Lord Ipsden," murmured the lovely Vere, "he used to be so nice, and do like everybody else. Mamma, I shall bring some work the next time."

"Do, my love."

PICNIC NO. 2.

In a house, two hundred yards from this scene, a merry dance, succeeding a merry song, had ended, and they were in the midst of an interesting story; Christie Johnstone was the narrator. She had found the tale in one of the viscount's books—it had made a great impression on her.

The rest were listening intently. In a room which had lately been all noise, not a sound was now to be heard but the narrator's voice.

"Aweel, lasses, here are the three wee kists set, the lads are to chuse—the ane that chuses reicht is to get Porsha, an' the lave to get the bag, and dee baitchelars—Flucker Johnstone, you that's sae clever—are ye for gowd, or siller, or leed?"

1st Fishwife. "Gowd for me!"

2d ditto. "The white siller's my taste."

Flucker. "Na! there's aye some deevelish trick in thir lassie's stories. I shall ha to, till the ither lads hae chused; the mair part will put themsels oot, ane will hit it off reicht maybe, then I shall gie him a hidin' an' carry off the lass. You-hoo!"

Jean Carnie. "That's you, Flucker."

Christie Johnstone. "And div ye really think we are gawn to let you see a' the world chuse? Na, lad, ye are putten oot o' the room, like witnesses."

Flucker. "Then I'd toss a penny; for gien ye trust to luck, she whiles favors ye, but gien ye commence to reason and argefy—ye're done!"

Christie. "The suitors had na your wit, my manny, or maybe they had na a penny to toss, sae ane chused the gowd, ane the siller; but they got an awfu' affront. The gold kist had just a skull intil't, and the siller a deed cuddy's head!"

Chorus of Females. "He! he! he!"

Ditto of Males. "Haw! haw! haw! haw! Ho!"

Christie. "An' Porsha puttit the pair of gowks to the door. Then came Bassanio, the lad fra Veeneece, that Porsha loed in secret. Veeneece, lasses, is a wonderful city; the streets o' 't are water, and the carriages are boats—that's in Chambers'."

Flucker. "Wha are ye making a fool o'?"

Christie. "What's wrang?"

Flucker. "Yon's just as big a lee as ever I heerd."

The words were scarcely out of his mouth ere he had reason to regret them; a severe box on the ear was administered by his indignant sister. Nobody pitied him.

Christie. "I'll laern yet' affront me before a' the company."

Jean Carnie. "Suppose it's a lee, there's nae silver to pay for it, Flucker."

Christie. "Jean, I never telt a lee in a' my days."

Jean. "There's ane to begin wi' then. Go ahead, Custy."

Christie. "She bade the music play for him, for music brightens thoucht; ony way, he chose the leed kist. Open'st and wasn't there Porsha's pictur, and a posy, that said:

'If you be well pleased with this, And hold your fortune for your bliss; Turn you where your leddy iss, And greet her wi' a loving—'" *(Pause).*

"Kess," roared the company.

Chorus, led by Flucker. "Hurraih!"

Christie (pathetically). "Flucker, behave!"

Sandy Liston (drunk). "Hur-raih!" He then solemnly reflected. "Na! but it's na hurraih, decency requires amen first an' hurraih afterward; here's kissin plenty, but I hear nae word o' the minister. Ye'll obsairve, young woman, that kissin's the prologue to sin, and I'm a decent mon, an' a gray-headed mon, an' your licht stories are no for me; sae if the minister's no expeckit I shall retire—an' tak my quiet gill my lane."

Jean Carnie. "And div ye really think a decent cummer like Custy wad let the lad and lass misbehave thirsels? Na! lad, the minister's at the door, but" (sinking her voice to a confidential whisper) "I daurna let him in, for fear he'd see ye hae putten the enemy in your mooth sae aerly. (That's Custy's word.)"

"Jemmy Drysel," replied Sandy, addressing vacancy, for Jemmy was mysteriously at work in the kitchen, "ye hae gotten a thoughtfu' wife." (Then, with a strong revulsion of feeling.) "Dinna let the blackguard* in here," cried he, "to spoil the young folk's sporrt."

* At present this is a spondee in England—a trochee in Scotland The pronunciation of this important word ought to be fixed, representing, as it does, so large a portion of the community in both countries.

Christie. "Aweel, lassies, comes a letter to Bassanio; he reads it, and turns as pale as deeth."

A Fishwife. "Gude help us."

Christie. "Poorsha behooved to ken his grief, wha had a better reicht? 'Here's a letter, leddy,' says he, 'the paper's the boedy of my freend, like, and every word in it a gaping wound.'"

A Fisherman. "Maircy on us."

Christie. "Lad, it was fra puir Antonio, ye mind o' him, Lasses. Hech! the ill luck o' yon man, no a ship come hame; ane foundered at sea, coming fra Tri-po-lis; the pirates scuttled another, an' ane ran ashore on the Goodwins, near Bright-helm-stane, that's in England itsel', I daur say. Sae he could na pay the three thoosand ducats, an' Shylock had grippit him, an' sought the pund o' flesh aff the breest o' him, puir body."

Sandy Liston. "He would na be the waur o' a wee bit hiding, yon thundering urang-utang; let the man alane, ye cursed old cannibal."

Christie. "Poorsha keepit her man but ae hoor till they were united, an' then sent him wi' a puckle o' her ain siller to Veeneece, and Antonio—think o' that, lassies—pairted on their wedding-day."

Lizzy Johnstone, a Fishwife, aged 12. "Hech! hech! it's lamentable."

Jean Carnie. "I'm saying, mairriage is quick wark, in some pairts—here there's an awfu' trouble to get a man."

A young Fishwife. "Ay, is there."

Omnes. "Haw! haw! haw!" (The fish-wife hides.)

Christie. "Fill your taupsels, lads and lasses, and awa to Veneece."

Sandy Liston (sturdily). "I'll no gang to sea this day."

Christie. "Noo, we are in the hall o' judgment. Here are set the judges, awfu' to behold; there, on his throne, presides the Juke."

Flucker. "She's awa to her Ennglish."

Lizzy Johnstone. "Did we come to Veeneece to speak Scoetch, ye useless fule?"

Christie. "Here, pale and hopeless, but resigned, stands the broken mairchant, Antonio; there, wi scales and knives, and revenge in his murderin' eye, stands the crewel Jew Shylock."

"Aweel," muttered Sandy, considerately, "I'll no mak a disturbance on a wedding day."

Christie. "They wait for Bell—I dinna mind his mind—a laerned lawyer, ony way; he's sick, but sends ane mair laerned still, and, when this ane comes, he looks not older nor wiser than mysel."

Flucker. "No possible!"

Christie. "Ye needna be sae sarcy, Flucker, for when he comes to his wark he soon lets 'em ken—runs his een like lightening ower the boend. 'This bond's forfeit. Is Antonio not able to dischairge the money?' 'Ay!' cries Bassanio, 'here's the sum thrice told.' Says the young judge in a bit whisper to Shylock, 'Shylock, there's thrice thy money offered thee. Be mairceful,' says he, out loud. 'Wha'll mak me?' says the Jew body. 'Mak ye!' says he; 'maircy is no a thing ye strain through a sieve, mon; it droppeth like the gentle dew fra' heaven upon the place beneath; it blesses him that gives and him that taks; it becomes the king better than his throne, and airthly power is maist like God's power when maircy seasons justice.'"

Robert Haw, Fisherman. "Dinna speak like that to me, onybody, or I shall gie ye my boat, and fling my nets intil it, as ye sail awa wi' her."

Jean Carnie. "Sae he let the puir deevil go. Oh! ye ken wha could stand up against siccan a shower o' Ennglish as thaat."

Christie. "He just said, 'My deeds upon my heed. I claim the law,' says he; 'there is no power in the tongue o' man to alter me. I stay here on my boend.'"

Sandy Liston. "I hae sat quiet!—quiet I hae sat against my will, no to disturb Jamie Drysel's weddin'; but ye carry the game ower far, Shylock, my lad. I'll just give yon bluidy-minded urang-utang a hidin', and bring Tony off, the gude, puir-spirited creature. And him, an' me, an' Bassanee, an' Porshee, we'll all hae a gill thegither."

He rose, and was instantly seized by two of the company, from whom he burst furiously, after a struggle, and the next moment was heard to fall clean from the top to the bottom of the stairs. Flucker and Jean ran out; the rest appealed against the interruption.

Christie. "Hech! he's killed. Sandy Liston's brake his neck."

"What aboot it, lassy?" said a young fisherman; "it's Antonio I'm feared for; save him, lassy, if poessible; but I doot ye'll no get him clear o' yon deevelich heathen.

"Auld Sandy's cheap sairved," added he, with all the indifference a human tone could convey.

"Oh, Cursty," said Lizzie Johnstone, with a peevish accent, "dinna break the bonny yarn for naething."

Flucker (returning). "He's a' reicht."

Christie. "Is he no dead?"

Flucker. "Him deed? he's sober—that's a' the change I see."

Christie. "Can he speak? I'm asking ye."

Flucker. "Yes, he can speak."

Christie. "What does he say, puir body?"

Flucker. "He sat up, an' sought a gill fra' the wife—puir body!"

Christie. "Hech! hech! he was my pupil in the airt o' sobriety!—aweel, the young judge rises to deliver the sentence of the coort. Silence!" thundered Christie. A lad and a lass that were slightly flirting were discountenanced.

Christie. "'A pund o' that same mairchant's flesh is thine! the coort awards it, and the law does give it.'"

A young Fishwife. "There, I thoucht sae; he's gaun to cut him, he's gaun to cut him; I'll no can bide." *(Exibat.)*

Christie. "There's a fulish goloshen. 'Have by a doctor to stop the blood.'—'I see nae doctor in the boend,' says the Jew body."

Flucker. "Bait your hook wi' a boend, and ye shall catch yon carle's saul, Satin, my lad."

Christie (with dismal pathos). "Oh, Flucker, dinna speak evil o' deegneties—that's maybe fishing for yoursel' the noo!—'An' ye shall cut the flesh frae off his breest.'—'A sentence,' says Shylock, 'come, prepare.'"

Christie made a dash *en Shylock,* and the company trembled.

Christie. "'Bide a wee,' says the judge, 'this boend gies ye na a drap o' bluid; the words expressly are, a pund o' flesh!'"

(A Dramatic Pause.)

Jean Carnie (drawing her breath). "That's into your mutton, Shylock"

Christie (with dismal pathos). "Oh, Jean! yon's an awfu' voolgar exprassion to come fra' a woman's mooth."

"Could ye no hae said, 'intil his bacon'?" said Lizzie Johnstone, confirming the remonstrance.

Christie. "'Then tak your boend, an' your pund o' flesh, but in cutting o' 't, if thou dost shed one drop of Christian bluid, thou diest!'"

Jean Carnie. "Hech!"

Christie. "'Thy goods are by the laws Veneece con-fis-cate, confiscate!'"

Then, like an artful narrator, she began to wind up the story more rapidly.

"Sae Shylock got to be no sae saucy. 'Pay the boend thrice,' says he, 'and let the puir deevil go.'—'Here it's,' says Bassanio.—Na! the young judge wadna let him.—'He has refused it in open coort; no a bawbee for Shylock but just the forfeiture; an' he daur na tak it.'—'I'm awa',' says he. 'The deivil tak ye a'.'—Na! he wasna to win clear sae; ance they'd gotten the Jew on the hep, they worried him, like good Christians, that's a fact. The judge fand a law that fitted him, for conspiring against the life of a citizen; an' he behooved to give up hoose an' lands, and be a Christian; yon was a soor drap—he tarned no weel, puir auld villain, an' scairtit; an' the lawyers sent ane o' their weary parchments till his hoose, and the puir auld heathen signed awa' his siller, an' Abraham, an' Isaac, an' Jacob, on the heed o' 't. I pity him, an auld, auld man; and his dochter had rin off wi' a Christian lad—they ca' her Jessica, and didn't she steal his very diamond ring that his ain lass gied him when he was young, an' maybe no sae hard-hairted?"

Jean Carnie. "Oh, the jaud! suppose he was a Jew, it was na her business to clean him oot."

A young Fishwife. "Aweel, it was only a Jew body, that's my comfort."

Christie. "Ye speak as a Jew was na a man; has not a Jew eyes, if ye please?"

Lizzy Johnstone. "Ay, has he!—and the awfuest lang neb atween 'em."

Christie. "Has not a Jew affections, paassions, organs?"

Jean. "Na! Christie; thir lads comes fr' Italy!"

Christie. "If you prick him, does he not bleed? if you tickle him, does na he lauch?"

A young Fishwife (pertly). "I never kittlet a Jew, for my pairt—sae I'll no can tell ye."

Christie. "If you poison him, does he not die? and if you wrang him" (with fury) "shall he not revenge?"

Lizzie Johnstone. "Oh! but ye're a fearsome lass."

Christie. "Wha'll give me a sang for my bonny yarn?"

Lord Ipsden, who had been an unobserved auditor of the latter part of the tale, here inquired whether she had brought her book.

"What'n buik?"

"Your music-book!"

"Here's my music-book," said Jean, roughly tapping her head.

"And here's mines," said Christie, birdly, touching her bosom.

"Richard," said she, thoughtfully, "I wish ye may no hae been getting in voolgar company. Div ye think we hae minds like rinning water?"

Flucker (avec malice). "And tongues like the mill-clack abune it? Because if ye think sae, captain—ye're no far wrang!"

Christie. "Na! we hae na muckle gowd maybe; but our minds are gowden vessels."

Jean. "Aha! lad."

Christie. "They are not saxpenny sieves, to let music an' meter through, and leave us none the wiser or better. Dinna gang in low voolgar company, or you a lost laddy."

Ipsden. "Vulgar, again! everybody has a different sense for that word, I think. What is vulgar?"

Christie. "Voolgar folk sit on an chair, ane, twa, whiles three hours, eatin' an' abune drinkin', as still as hoegs, or gruntin' puir every-day clashes, goessip, rubbich; when ye are aside them, ye might as weel be aside a cuddy; they canna gie ye a sang, they canna gie ye a story, they canna think ye a thoucht, to save their useless lives; that's voolgar folk."

She sings. "A caaller herrin'!"

Jean. "A caaller herrin'!"

Omnes.

"Come buy my bonny caaller herrin', Six a penny caaller from the sea," etc.

The music chimed in, and the moment the song was done, without pause, or anything to separate or chill the succession of the arts, the fiddles diverged with a gallant plunge into "The Dusty Miller." The dancers found their feet by an instinct as rapid, and a rattling reel shook the floor like thunder. Jean Carnie assumed the privilege of a bride, and seized his lordship; Christie, who had a mind to dance with him too, took Flucker captive, and these four were one reel! There were seven others.

The principle of reel dancing is articulation; the foot strikes the ground for every *accented* note (and, by the by, it is their weakness of accent which makes all English reel and hornpipe players such failures).

And in the best steps of all, which it has in common with the hornpipe, such as the quick "heel and toe," "the sailor's fling," and the "double shuffle," the foot strikes the ground for every *single* note of the instrument.

All good dancing is beautiful.

But this articulate dancing, compared with the loose, lawless diffluence of motion that goes by that name, gives me (I must confess it) as much more pleasure as articulate singing is superior to tunes played on the voice by a young lady:

Or the clean playing of my mother to the piano-forte splashing of my daughter; though the latter does attack the instrument as a washerwoman her soapsuds, and the former works like a lady.

Or skating to sliding:

Or English verse to dactyls in English:

Or painting to daubing:

Or preserved strawberries to strawberry jam.

What says Goldsmith of the two styles? "They swam, sprawled, frisked, and languished; but Olivia's foot was as pat to the music as its echo."—*Vicar of Wakefield.*

Newhaven dancing aims also at fun; laughter mingles with agility; grotesque yet graceful gestures are flung in, and little inspiring cries flung out.

His lordship soon entered into the spirit of it. Deep in the mystery of the hornpipe, he danced one or two steps Jean and Christie had never seen, but their eyes were instantly on his feet, and they caught in a minute and executed these same steps.

To see Christie Johnstone do the double-shuffle with her arms so saucily akimbo, and her quick elastic foot at an angle of forty-five, was a treat.

The dance became inspiriting, inspiring, intoxicating; and, when the fiddles at last left off, the feet went on another seven bars by the enthusiastic impulse.

And so, alternately spinning yarns, singing songs, dancing, and making fun, and mingling something of heart and brain in all, these benighted creatures made themselves happy instead of peevish, and with a day of stout, vigorous, healthy pleasure, refreshed, indemnified, and warmed themselves for many a day of toil.

Such were the two picnics of Inch Coombe, and these rival cliques, agreeing in nothing else, would have agreed in this: each, if allowed (but we won't allow either) to judge the other, would have pronounced the same verdict:

"Ils ne savent pas vivre ces gens-l'a."

CHAPTER XI

Two of our personages left Inch Coombe less happy than when they came to it.

Lord Ipsden encountered Lady Barbara with Mr.—, who had joined her upon the island.

He found them discoursing, as usual, about the shams of the present day, and the sincerity of Cromwell and Mahomet, and he found himself *de trop.*

They made him, for the first time, regret the loss of those earnest times when, "to avoid the inconvenience of both addressing the same lady," you could cut a rival's throat at once, and be smiled on by the fair and society.

That a book-maker should blaspheme high civilization, by which alone he exists, and one of whose diseases and flying pains he is, neither surprised nor moved him; but that any human being's actions should be affected by such tempestuous twaddle was ridiculous.

And that the witty Lady Barbara should be caught by this chaff was intolerable; he began to feel bitter.

He had the blessings of the poor, the good opinion of the

world; every living creature was prepossessed in his favor but one, and that one despised him; it was a diabolical prejudice; it was the spiteful caprice of his fate.

His heart, for a moment, was in danger of deteriorating. He was miserable; the Devil suggested to him, "make others miserable too;" and he listened to the advice.

There was a fine breeze, but instead of sailing on a wind, as he might have done, he made a series of tacks, and all were ill.

The earnest man first; and Flucker announced the skipper's insanity to the whole town of Newhaven, for, of course, these tacks were all marine solecisms.

The other discontented Picnician was Christie Johnstone. Gatty never came; and this, coupled with five or six days' previous neglect, could no longer pass unnoticed.

Her gayety failed her before the afternoon was ended; and the last two hours were spent by her alone, watching the water on all sides for him.

At last, long after the departure of his lordship's yacht, the Newhaven boat sailed from Inch Coombe with the wedding party. There was now a strong breeze, and the water every now and then came on board. So the men set the foresail with two reefs, and drew the mainsail over the women; and there, as they huddled together in the dark, Jean Carnie discovered that our gay story-teller's eyes were wet with tears.

Jean said nothing; she embraced her; and made them flow faster.

Charles Reade

But, when they came alongside the pier, Jean, who was the first to get her head from under the sail, whipped it back again and said to Christie:

"Here he is, Christie; dinna speak till him."

And sure enough there was, in the twilight, with a pale face and an uneasy look—Mr. Charles Gatty!

He peered timidly into the boat, and, when he saw Christie, an "Ah!" that seemed to mean twenty different things at once, burst from his bosom. He held out his arm to assist her.

She cast on him one glance of mute reproach, and, placing her foot on the boat's gunwale, sprang like an antelope upon the pier, without accepting his assistance.

Before going further, we must go back for this boy, and conduct him from where we left him up to the present point.

The moment he found himself alone with Jean Carnie, in his own house, he began to tell her what trouble he was in; how his mother had convinced him of his imprudence in falling in love with Christie Johnstone; and how she insisted on a connection being broken off which had given him his first glimpse of heaven upon earth, and was contrary to common sense.

Jean heard him out, and then, with the air of a lunatic-asylum keeper to a rhodomontading patient, told him "he was one fool, and his mother was another." First she took him up on the score of prudence.

"You," said she, "are a beggarly painter, without a rap; Christie has houses, boats, nets, and money; you are in debt; she lays by money every week. It is not prudent on her part to take up with you—the better your bargain, my lad."

Under the head of common sense, which she maintained was all on the same side of the question, she calmly inquired:

"How could an old woman of sixty be competent to judge how far human happiness depends on love, when she has no experience of that passion, and the reminiscences of her youth have become dim and dark? You might as well set a judge in court, that has forgotten the law—common sense," said she, "the old wife is sixty, and you are twenty—what can she do for you the forty years you may reckon to outlive her? Who is to keep you through those weary years but the wife of your own choice, not your mother's? You English does na read the Bible, or ye'd ken that a lad is to 'leave his father and mother, and cleave until his wife,'" added she; then with great contempt she repeated, "common sense, indeed! ye're fou wi' your common sense; ye hae the name o' 't pat eneuch—but there's na muckle o' that mairchandise in your harns."

Gatty was astonished. What! was there really common sense on the side of bliss? and when Jean told him to join her party at Inch Coombe, or never look her in the face again, scales seemed to fall from his eyes; and, with a heart that turned in a moment from lead to a feather, he vowed he would be at Inch Coombe.

He then begged Jean on no account to tell Christie the struggle he had been subjected to, since his scruples were now entirely conquered.

Jean acquiesced at once, and said: "Indeed, she would be very sorry to give the lass that muckle pain."

She hinted, moreover, that her neebor's spirit was so high,

she was quite capable of breaking with him at once upon such an intimation; and she, Jean, was "nae mischief-maker."

In the energy of his gratitude, he kissed this dark-browed beauty, professing to see in her a sister.

And she made no resistance to this way of showing gratitude, but muttered between her teeth, "He's just a bairn!"

And so she went about her business.

On her retreat, his mother returned to him, and, with a sad air, hoped nothing that that rude girl had said had weakened his filial duty.

"No, mother," said he.

She then, without explaining how she came acquainted with Jean's arguments, proceeded to demolish them one by one.

"If your mother is old and experienced," said she, "benefit by her age and experience. She has not forgotten love, nor the ills it leads to, when not fortified by prudence. Scripture says a man shall cleave to his wife when he has left his parents; but in making that, the most important step of life, where do you read that he is to break the fifth commandment? But I do you wrong, Charles, you never could have listened to that vulgar girl when she told you your mother was not your best friend."

"N—no, mother, of course not."

"Then you will not go to that place to break my heart, and undo all you have done this week."

"I should like to go, mother."

"You will break my heart if you do."

"Christie will feel herself slighted, and she has not deserved this treatment from me."

"The other will explain to her, and if she is as good a girl as you say—"

"She is an angel!"

"How can a fishwife be an angel? Well, then, she will not set a son to disobey his mother."

"I don't think she would! but is all the goodness to be on her side?"

"No, Charles, you do your part; deny yourself, be an obedient child, and your mother's blessing and the blessing of Heaven will rest upon you."

In short, he was not to go to Inch Coombe.

He stayed at home, his mother set him to work; he made a poor hand of it, he was so wretched. She at last took compassion on him, and in the evening, when it was now too late for a sail to Inch Coombe, she herself recommended a walk to him.

The poor boy's feet took him toward Newhaven, not that he meant to go to his love, but he could not forbear from looking at the place which held her.

He was about to return, when a spacious blue jacket hailed him. Somewhere inside this jacket was Master Flucker, who had returned in the yacht, leaving his sister on the island.

Gatty instantly poured out a flood of questions.

The baddish boy reciprocated fluency. He informed him "that his sister had been the star of a goodly company, and that, her own lad having stayed away, she had condescended to make a conquest of the skipper himself.

"He had come in quite at the tag-end of one of her stories, but it had been sufficient to do his business—he had danced with her, had even whistled while she sung. (Hech, it was bonny!)

"And when the cutter sailed, he, Flucker, had seen her perched on a rock, like a mermaid, watching their progress, which had been slow, because the skipper, infatuated with so sudden a passion, had made a series of ungrammatical tacks."

"For his part he was glad," said the gracious Flucker; "the lass was a prideful hussy, that had given some twenty lads a sore heart and him many a sore back; and he hoped his skipper, with whom he naturally identified himself rather than with his sister, would avenge the male sex upon her."

In short, he went upon this tack till he drove poor Gatty nearly mad.

Here was a new feeling superadded; at first he felt injured, but on reflection what cause of complaint had he?

He had neglected her; he might have been her partner—he had left her to find one where she could.

Fool, to suppose that so beautiful a creature would ever be neglected—except by him!

It was more than he could bear.

He determined to see her, to ask her forgiveness, to tell her everything, to beg her to decide, and, for his part, he would abide by her decision.

Christie Johnstone, as we have already related, declined his arm, sprang like a deer upon the pier, and walked toward her home, a quarter of a mile distant.

Gatty followed her, disconsolately, hardly knowing what to do.

At last, observing that she drew near enough to the wall to allow room for another on the causeway, he had just nous enough to creep alongside and pull her sleeve somewhat timidly.

"Christie, I want to speak to you:"

"What can ye hae to say till me?"

"Christie, I am very unhappy; and I want to tell you why, but I have hardly the strength or the courage."

"Ye shall come ben my hoose if ye are unhappy, and we'll hear your story; come away.

He had never been admitted into her house before.

They found it clean as a snowdrift.

They found a bright fire, and Flucker frying innumerable steaks.

The baddish boy had obtained them in his sister's name and

Charles Reade

at her expense, at the flesher's, and claimed credit for his affection.

Potatoes he had boiled in their jackets, and so skillfully, that those jackets hung by a thread.

Christie laid an unbleached table-cloth, that somehow looked sweeter than a white one, as brown bread is sweeter than white.

But lo! Gatty could not eat; so then Christie would not, because he refused her cheer.

The baddish boy chuckled, and addressed himself to the nice brown steaks with their rich gravy.

On such occasions a solo on the knife and fork seemed better than a trio to the gracious Flucker.

Christie moved about the room, doing little household matters; Gatty's eye followed her.

Her beauty lost nothing in this small apartment; she was here, like a brilliant in some quaint, rough setting, which all earth's jewelers should despise, and all its poets admire, and it should show off the stone and not itself.

Her beauty filled the room, and almost made the spectators ill.

Gatty asked himself whether he could really have been such a fool as to think of giving up so peerless a creature.

Suddenly an idea occurred to him, a bright one, and not inconsistent with a true artist's character—he would decline to act in so doubtful a case. He would float passively down the tide of events—he would neither desert her, nor disobey his mother; he would take everything as it came, and to begin, as he was there, he would for the present say nothing but what he felt, and what he felt was that he loved her.

He told her so accordingly.

She replied, concealing her satisfaction, "that, if he liked her, he would not have refused to eat when she asked him."

But our hero's appetite had returned with his change of purpose, and he instantly volunteered to give the required proof of affection.

Accordingly two pound of steaks fell before him. Poor boy, he had hardly eaten a genuine meal for a week past.

Christie sat opposite him, and every time he looked off his plate he saw her rich blue eyes dwelling on him.

Everything contributed to warm his heart, he yielded to the spell, he became contented, happy, gay.

Flucker ginger-cordialed him, his sister bewitched him.

She related the day's events in a merry mood.

Mr. Gatty burst forth into singing.

He sung two light and somber trifles, such as in the present day are deemed generally encouraging to spirits, and particularly in accordance with the sentiment of supper— they were about Death and Ivy Green.

The dog's voice was not very powerful, but sweet and round as honey dropping from the comb.

His two hearers were entranced, for the creature sang with an inspiration good singers dare not indulge.

He concluded by informing Christie that the ivy was symbolical of her, and the oak prefigured Charles Gatty, Esq.

He might have inverted the simile with more truth.

In short, he never said a word to Christie about parting with her, but several about being buried in the same grave with her, sixty years hence, for which the spot he selected was Westminster Abbey.

And away he went, leaving golden opinions behind him.

The next day Christie was so affected with his conduct, coming as it did after an apparent coolness, that she conquered her bashfulness and called on the "vile count," and with some blushes and hesitation inquired, "Whether a painter lad was a fit subject of charity."

"Why not?" said his lordship.

She told him Gatty's case, and he instantly promised to see that artist's pictures, particularly an "awfu' bonny ane;" the hero of which she described as an English minister blessing the bairns with one hand, and giving orders to kill the puir Scoetch with the other.

"C'est e'gal," said Christie in Scotch, "it's awfu' bonny."

Gatty reached home late; his mother had retired to rest.

But the next morning she drew from him what had happened, and then ensued another of those dialogues which I am ashamed again to give the reader.

Suffice it to say, that she once more prevailed, though with far greater difficulty; time was to be given him to unsew a connection which he could not cut asunder, and he, with tearful eyes and a heavy heart, agreed to take some step the very first opportunity.

This concession was hardly out of his mouth, ere his mother made him kneel down and bestowed her blessing upon him.

He received it coldly and dully, and expressed a languid hope it might prove a charm to save him from despair; and sad, bitter, and dejected, forced himself to sit down and work on the picture that was to meet his unrelenting creditor's demand.

He was working on his picture, and his mother, with her needle, at the table, when a knock was heard, and gay as a lark, and fresh as the dew on the shamrock, Christie Johnstone stood in person in the apartment.

She was evidently the bearer of good tidings; but, before she could express them, Mrs. Gatty beckoned her son aside, and announcing, "she should be within hearing," bade him take the occasion that so happily presented itself, and make the first step.

At another time, Christie, who had learned from Jean the arrival of Mrs. Gatty, would have been struck with the old lady's silence; but she came to tell the depressed painter that the charitable viscount was about to visit him and his picture; and she was so full of the good fortune likely to ensue, that she was neglectful of minor considerations.

It so happened, however, that certain interruptions prevented her from ever delivering herself of the news in question.

First, Gatty himself came to her, and, casting uneasy glances at the door by which his mother had just gone out, said:

"Christie!"

"My lad!"

"I want to paint your likeness."

This was for a *souvenir,* poor fellow!

"Hech! I wad like fine to be painted."

"It must be exactly the same size as yourself, and so like you, that, should we be parted, I may seem not to be quite alone in the world."

Here he was obliged to turn his head away.

"But we'll no pairt," replied Christie, cheerfully. "Suppose ye're puir, I'm rich, and it's a' one; dinna be so cast down for auchty pund."

At this, a slipshod servant entered, and said: "There's a fisher lad, inquiring for Christie Johnstone."

"It will be Flucker," said Christie; "show him ben. What's wrang the noo I wonder!"

The baddish boy entered, took up a position and remained apparently passive, hands in pockets.

Christie. "Aweel, what est?"

Flucker. "Custy."

Christie. "What's your will, my manny?"

Flucker. "Custy, I was at Inch Keith the day."

Christie. "And hae ye really come to Edinbro' to tell me thaat?"

Flucker (dryly). "Oh! ye ken the lasses are a hantle wiser than we are—will ye hear me? South Inch Keith, I played a bowl i' the water, just for divairsion—and I catched twarree fish!"

Christie. "Floonders, I bet."

Flucker. "Does floonders swim high? I'll let you see his gills, and if ye are a reicht fishwife ye'll smell bluid."

Here he opened his jacket, and showed a bright little fish.

In a moment all Christie's nonchalance gave way to a fiery animation. She darted to Flucker's side.

"Ye hae na been sae daft as tell?" asked she.

Flucker shook his head contemptuously.

"Ony birds at the island, Flucker?"

"Sea-maws, plenty, and a bird I dinna ken; he moonted sae high, then doon like thunder intil the sea, and gart the water flee as high as Haman, and porpoises as big as my boat."

"Porr-poises, fulish laddy—ye hae seen the herrin whale at his wark, and the solant guse ye hae seen her at wark; and beneath the sea, Flucker, every coedflsh and doegfish, and fish that has teeth, is after them; and half Scotland wad be at

Inch Keith Island if they kenned what ye hae tell't me—dinna speak to me."

During this, Gatty, who did not comprehend this sudden excitement, or thought it childish, had tried in vain to win her attention.

At last he said, a little peevishly, "Will you not attend to me, and tell me at least when you will sit to me?"

Set!" cried she. "When there's nae wark to be done stanning."

And with this she was gone.

At the foot of the stairs, she said to her brother:

"Puir lad! I'll sune draw auchty punds fra' the sea for him, with my feyther's nets."

As she disappeared, Mrs. Gatty appeared. "And this is the woman whose mind was not in her dirty business," cried she. "Does not that open your eyes, Charles?"

"Ah! Charles," added she, tenderly, "there's no friend like a mother."

And off she carried the prize—his vanity had been mortified.

And so that happened to Christie Johnstone which has befallen many a woman—the greatness of her love made that love appear small to her lover.

"Ah! mother," cried he, "I must live for you and my art; I am not so dear to her as I thought."

And so, with a sad heart, he turned away from her; while she, with a light heart, darted away to think and act for him.

CHAPTER XII

IT was some two hours after this that a gentleman, plainly dressed, but whose clothes seemed a part of himself (whereas mine I have observed hang upon me; and the Rev. Josiah Splitall's stick to him)—glided into the painter's room, with an inquiry whether he had not a picture or two disposable.

"I have one finished picture, sir," said the poor boy; "but the price is high!"

He brought it, in a faint-hearted way; for he had shown it to five picture-dealers, and all five agreed it was hard.

He had painted a lime-tree, distant fifty yards, and so painted it that it looked something like a lime-tree fifty yards off.

"That was *mesquin,*" said his judges; "the poetry of painting required abstract trees, at metaphysical distance, not the various trees of nature, as they appear under positive accidents."

On this Mr. Gatty had deluged them with words.

"When it is art, truth, or sense to fuse a cow, a horse, and a critic into one undistinguishable quadruped, with six legs, then it will be art to melt an ash, an elm, and a lime, things that differ more than quadrupeds, into what you call abstract trees, that any man who has seen a tree, as well as looked at one, would call drunken stinging-nettles. You, who never look at nature, how can you judge the arts, which are all but copies of nature? At two hundred yards' distance, full-grown trees are more distinguishable than the animal tribe. Paint me an abstract human being, neither man nor a woman," said he, "and then I will agree to paint a tree that shall be no tree; and, if no man will buy it, perhaps the father of lies will take it off my hands, and hang it in the only place it would not disgrace."

In short, he never left off till he had crushed the non-buyers with eloquence and satire; but he could not crush them into buyers—they beat him at the passive retort.

Poor Gatty, when the momentary excitement of argument had subsided, drank the bitter cup all must drink awhile, whose bark is alive and strong enough to stem the current down which the dead, weak things of the world are drifting, many of them into safe harbors.

And now he brought out his picture with a heavy heart.

"Now," said he to himself, "this gentleman will talk me dead, and leave me no richer in coin, and poorer in time and patience."

The picture was placed in a light, the visitor sat down before it.

A long pause ensued.

"Has he fainted?" thought Gatty, ironically; "he doesn't gabble."

"If you do not mind painting before me," said the visitor, "I should be glad if you would continue while I look into this picture."

Gatty painted.

The visitor held his tongue.

At first the silence made the artist uneasy, but by degrees it began to give him pleasure; whoever this was, it was not one of the flies that had hitherto stung him, nor the jackdaws that had chattered him dead.

Glorious silence! he began to paint under its influence like one inspired.

Half an hour passed thus.

"What is the price of this work of art?"

"Eighty pounds."

"I take it," said his visitor, quietly.

What, no more difficulty than that? He felt almost disappointed at gaining his object so easily.

"I am obliged to you, sir; much obliged to you," he added, for he reflected what eighty pounds were to him just then.

"It is my descendants who are obliged to you," replied the gentleman; "the picture is immortal!"

These words were an epoch in the painter's life.

The grave, silent inspection that had preceded them, the cool, deliberate, masterly tone in which they were said, made them oracular to him.

Words of such import took him by surprise.

He had thirsted for average praise in vain.

A hand had taken him, and placed him at the top of the tree.

He retired abruptly, or he would have burst into tears.

He ran to his mother.

"Mother," said he, "I am a painter; I always thought so at bottom, but I suppose it is the height of my ideas makes me discontented with my work."

"What has happened?'

"There is a critic in my room. I had no idea there was a critic in the creation, and there is one in my room.

"Has he bought your picture, my poor boy?" said Mrs. Gatty, distrustfully.

To her surprise he replied:

"Yes! he has got it; only eighty pounds for an immortal picture."

Mrs. Gatty was overjoyed, Gatty was a little sad; but, reviving, he professed himself glad; the picture was going to a judge.

"It is not much money," said he, "but the man has spoken words that are ten thousand pounds to me."

He returned to the room; his visitor, hat in hand, was about to go; a few words were spoken about the art of painting, this led to a conversation, and then to a short discussion.

The newcomer soon showed Mr. Charles Gatty his ignorance of facts.

This man had sat quietly before a multitude of great pictures, new and old, in England.

He cooled down Charles Gatty, Esq., monopolist of nature and truth.

He quoted to him thirty painters in Germany, who paint every stroke of a landscape in the open air, and forty in various nations who had done it in times past.

"You, sir," he went on, "appear to hang on the skirts of a certain clique, who handle the brush well, but draw ill, and look at nature through the spectacles of certain ignorant painters who spoiled canvas four hundred years ago.

"Go no further in that direction.

"Those boys, like all quacks, have one great truth which they disfigure with more than one falsehood.

"Hold fast their truth, which is a truth the world has always possessed, though its practice has been confined to the honest and laborious few.

"Eschew their want of mind and taste.

"Shrink with horror from that profane *culte de laideur,* that 'love of the lopsided,' they have recovered from the foul receptacles of decayed art."

He reminded him further, that "Art is not imitation, but illusion; that a plumber and glazier of our day and a medieval painter are more alike than any two representatives of general styles that can be found; and for the same reason, namely, that with each of these art is in its infancy; these two sets of bunglers have not learned how to produce the illusions of art."

To all this he added a few words of compliment on the mind, as well as mechanical dexterity, of the purchased picture, bade him good morning, and glided away like a passing sunbeam.

"A mother's blessing is a great thing to have, and to deserve," said Mrs. Gatty, who had rejoined her son.

"It is, indeed," said Charles. He could not help being struck by the coincidence.

He had made a sacrifice to his mother, and in a few hours one of his troubles had melted away.

In the midst of these reflections arrived Mr. Saunders with a note.

The note contained a check for one hundred and fifty pounds, with these lines, in which the writer excused himself for the amendment: "I am a painter myself," said he, "and it is impossible that eighty pounds can remunerate the time expended on this picture, to say nothing of the skill."

We have treated this poor boy's picture hitherto with just contempt, but now that it is gone into a famous collection, mind, we always admired it; we always said so, we take our oath we did; if we have hitherto deferred framing it, that was merely because it was not sold.

MR. GATTY'S PICTURE, AT PRESENT IN THE
COLLECTION OF LORD IPSDEN!

There was, hundreds of years ago, a certain Bishop of
Durham, who used to fight in person against the Scotch, and
defeat them. When he was not with his flock, the northern
wolves sometimes scattered it; but when the holy father was
there with his prayers and his battle-ax, England won the
day!

This nettled the Scottish king, so he penetrated one day, with
a large band, as far as Durham itself, and for a short time
blocked the prelate up in his stronghold. This was the period
of Mr. Gatty's picture.

Whose title was:

"Half Church of God, half Tower against the Scot."

In the background was the cathedral, on the towers of which
paced to and fro men in armor, with the western sun
glittering thereon. In the center, a horse and cart, led by a
boy, were carrying a sheaf of arrows, tied with a straw band.
In part of the foreground was the prelate, in a half suit of
armor, but bareheaded; he was turning away from the boy to
whom his sinking hand had indicated his way into the holy
castle, and his benignant glance rested on a child, whom its
mother was holding up for his benediction. In the foreground
the afternoon beams sprinkled gold on a long grassy slope,
corresponding to the elevation on which the cathedral stood,
separated by the river Wear from the group; and these calm
beauties of Nature, with the mother and child, were the
peaceful side of this twofold story.

Such are the dry details. But the soul of its charm no pen can
fling on paper. For the stately cathedral stood and lived; the

little leaves slumbered yet lived; and the story floated and lived, in the potable gold of summer afternoon.

To look at this painted poem was to feel a thrill of pleasure in bare existence; it went through the eyes, where paintings stop, and warmed the depths and recesses of the heart with its sunshine and its glorious air.

CHAPTER XIII

"WHAT is in the wind this dark night? Six Newhaven boats and twenty boys and hobbledehoys, hired by the Johnstones at half a crown each for a night's job."

"Secret service!"

"What is it for?"

"I think it is a smuggling lay," suggested Flucker, "but we shall know all in good time."

"Smuggling!" Their countenances fell; they had hoped for something more nearly approaching the illegal.

"Maybe she has fand the herrin'," said a ten-year-old.

"Haw! haw! haw!" went the others. "She find the herrin', when there's five hundred fishermen after them baith sides the Firrth."

The youngster was discomfited.

In fact the expedition bore no signs of fishing.

The six boats sailed at sundown, led by Flucker. He brought

to on the south side of Inch Keith, and nothing happened for about an hour.

Then such boys as were awake saw two great eyes of light coming up from Granton; rattle went the chain cable, and Lord Ipsden's cutter swung at anchor in four fathom water.

A thousand questions to Flucker.

A single puff of tobacco-smoke was his answer.

And now crept up a single eye of light from Leith; she came among the boats; the boys recognized a crazy old cutter from Leith harbor, with Christie Johnstone on board.

"What is that brown heap on her deck?"

"A mountain of nets—fifty stout herring-nets."

Tunc manifesta fides.

A yell burst from all the boys.

"He's gaun to tak us to Dunbar."

"Half a crown! ye're no blate."

Christie ordered the boats alongside her cutter, and five nets were dropped into each boat, six into Flucker's.

The depth of the water was given them, and they were instructed to shoot their nets so as to keep a fathom and a half above the rocky bottom.

A herring net is simply a wall of meshes twelve feet deep, fifty feet long; it sinks to a vertical position by the weight of net twine, and is kept from sinking to the bottom of the sea by bladders or corks. These nets are tied to one another, and paid out at the stern of the boat. Boat and nets drift with the tide; if, therefore, the nets touched the rocks they would be torn to pieces, and the fisherman ruined.

And this saves the herring—that fish lies hours and hours at the very bottom of the sea like a stone, and the poor fisherman shall drive with his nets a yard or two over a square mile of fish, and not catch a herring tail; on the other hand, if they rise to play for five minutes, in that five minutes they shall fill seven hundred boats.

At nine o'clock all the boats had shot their nets, and Christie went alongside his lordship's cutter; he asked her many questions about herring fishery, to which she gave clear answers, derived from her father, who had always been what the fishermen call a lucky fisherman; that is, he had opened his eyes and judged for himself.

Lord Ipsden then gave her blue lights to distribute among the boats, that the first which caught herring might signal all hands.

This was done, and all was expectation. Eleven o'clock came —no signal from any boat.

Christie became anxious. At last she went round to the boats; found the boys all asleep except the baddish boy; waked them up, and made them all haul in their first net. The nets came in as black as ink, no sign of a herring.

There was but one opinion; there was no herring at Inch Keith; they had not been there this seven years.

At last, Flucker, to whom she came in turn, told her he was

going into two fathom water, where he would let out the bladders and drop the nets on their cursed backs.

A strong remonstrance was made by Christie, but the baddish boy insisted that he had an equal right in all her nets, and, setting his sail, he ran into shoal water.

Christie began to be sorrowful; instead of making money, she was going to throw it away, and the ne'er-do-weel Flucker would tear six nets from the ropes.

Flucker hauled down his sail, and unstepped his mast in two fathom water; but he was not such a fool as to risk his six nets; he devoted one to his experiment, and did it well; he let out his bladder line a fathom, so that one half his net would literally be higgledy-piggledy with the rocks, unless the fish were there *en masse.*

No long time was required.

In five minutes he began to haul in the net; first, the boys hauled in the rope, and then the net began to approach the surface. Flucker looked anxiously down, the other lads incredulously; suddenly they all gave a yell of triumph—an appearance of silver and lightning mixed had glanced up from the bottom; in came the first two yards of the net— there were three herrings in it. These three proved Flucker's point as well as three million.

They hauled in the net. Before they had a quarter of it in, the net came up to the surface, and the sea was alive with molten silver. The upper half of the net was empty, but the lower half was one solid mass of fish.

The boys could not find a mesh, they had nothing to handle but fish.

At this moment the easternmost boat showed a blue light.

"The fish are rising," said Flucker, "we'll na risk nae mair nets."

Soon after this a sort of song was heard from the boat that had showed a light. Flucker, who had got his net in, ran down to her, and found, as he suspected, that the boys had not power to draw the weight of fish over the gunwale.

They were singing, as sailors do, that they might all pull together; he gave them two of his crew, and ran down to his own skipper.

The said skipper gave him four men.

Another blue light!

Christie and her crew came a little nearer the boats, and shot twelve nets.

The yachtsmen entered the sport with zeal, so did his lordship.

The boats were all full in a few minutes, and nets still out.

Then Flucker began to fear some of these nets would sink with the weight of fish; for the herring die after a while in a net, and a dead herring sinks.

What was to be done?

They got two boats alongside the cutter, and unloaded them into her as well as they could; but before they could half do this the other boats hailed them.

They came to one of them; the boys were struggling with a thing which no stranger would have dreamed was a net.

Imagine a white sheet, fifty feet long, varnished with red-hot silver. There were twenty barrels in this single net. By dint of fresh hands they got half of her in, and then the meshes began to break; the men leaned over the gunwale, and put their arms round blocks and masses of fish, and so flung them on board; and the codfish and dogfish snapped them almost out of the men's hands like tigers.

At last they came to a net which was a double wall of herring; it had been some time in the water, and many of the fish were dead; they tried their best, but it was impracticable; they laid hold of the solid herring, and when they lifted up a hundred-weight clear of the water, away it all tore, and sank back again.

They were obliged to cut away this net, with twenty pounds sterling in her. They cut away the twine from the head-ropes, and net and fish went to the bottom.

All hands were now about the cutter; Christie's nets were all strong and new; they had been some time in the water; in hauling them up her side, quantities of fish fell out of the net into the water, but there were enough left.

She averaged twelve barrels a net.

Such of the yawls as were not quite full crept between the cutter and the nets, and caught all they wanted.

The projector of this fortunate speculation suddenly announced that she was very sleepy.

Flucker rolled her up in a sail, and she slept the sleep of

Charles Reade

infancy on board her cutter.

When she awoke it was seven o'clock in the morning, and her cutter was creeping with a smart breeze about two miles an hour, a mile from Newhaven pier.

The yacht had returned to Granton, and the yawls, very low in the water, were creeping along like snails, with both sails set.

The news was in Edinburgh long before they landed. They had been discerned under Inch Keith at the dawn.

And the manner of their creeping along, when there was such a breeze, told the tale at once to the keen, experienced eyes that are sure to be scanning the sea.

Donkey-carts came rattling down from the capital.

Merchants came pelting down to Newhaven pier.

The whole story began to be put together by bits, and comprehended. Old Johnstone's cleverness was recalled to mind.

The few fishermen left at Newhaven were ready to kill themselves.

Their wives were ready to do the same good office for La Johnstone.

Four Irish merchants agreed to work together, and to make a show of competition, the better to keep the price down within bounds.

It was hardly fair, four men against one innocent

unguarded female.

But this is a wicked world.

Christie landed, and proceeded to her own house; on the way she was met by Jean Carnie, who debarrassed her of certain wrappers, and a handkerchief she had tied round her head, and informed her she was the pride of Newhaven.

She next met these four little merchants, one after another.

And since we ought to dwell as little as possible upon scenes in which unguarded innocence is exposed to artful conspiracies, we will put a page or two into the brute form of dramatic dialogue, and so sail through it quicker.

1st Merchant. "Where are ye going, Meggie?"

Christie Johnstone. "If onybody asks ye, say ye dinna ken."

1st Mer. "Will ye sell your fish?"

Christie. "Suner than gie them."

1st Mer. "You will be asking fifteen shillin' the cran."

Christie. "And ten to that."

1st Mer. "Good-morning."

2d Mer. "Would he not go over fifteen shillings? Oh, the thief o' the world!— I'll give sixteen."

3d Mer. "But I'll give eighteen."

2d Mer. "More fool you! Take him up, my girl."

Christie. "Twenty-five is my price the day."

3d Mer. "You will keep them till Sunday week and sell their bones."

[Exeunt the three Merchants. Enter 4th Merchant.

4th Mer. "Are your fish sold? I'll give sixteen shillings."

Christie. "I'm seeking twenty-five, an' I'm offered eighteen."

4th Mer. "Take it." *[Exit.]*

Christie. "They hae putten their heads thegither."

Here Flucker came up to her, and told her there was a Leith merchant looking for her. "And, Custy," said he, "there's plenty wind getting up, your fish will be sair hashed; put them off your hands, I rede ye."

Christie. "Ay, lad! Flucker, hide, an' when I play my hand sae, ye'll run in an cry, 'Cirsty, the Irishman will gie ye twenty-two schellin the cran.'"

Flucker. "Ye ken mair than's in the catecheesm, for as releegious as ye are."

The Leith merchant was Mr. Miller, and this is the way he worked.

Miller (in a mellifluous voice). "Are ye no fatigued, my deear?"

Christie (affecting fatigue). "Indeed, sir, and I am."

Miller. "Shall I have the pleasure to deal wi' ye?"

Christie. "If it's your pleasure, sir. I'm seekin' twenty-five schellin."

Miller (pretending not to hear). "As you are a beginner, I must offer fair; twenty schellin you shall have, and that's three shillings above Dunbar."

Christie. "Wad ye even carted herrin with my fish caller fra' the sea? and Dunbar—oh, fine! ye ken there's nae herrin at Dunbar the morn; this is the Dunbar schule that slipped westward. I'm the matirket, ye'll hae to buy o' me or gang to your bed" *(here she signaled to Flucker).* "I'll no be oot o' mine lang."

Enter Flucker hastily, crying: "Cirsty, the Irishman will gie ye twenty-two schellin."

"I'll no tak it," said Christie.

"They are keen to hae them," said Flucker; and hastily retired, as if to treat further with the small merchants.

On this, Mr. Miller, pretending to make for Leith, said, carelessly, "Twenty-three shillings, or they are not for me."

"Tak the cutter's freight at a hundre' cran, an' I'm no caring," said Christie.

"They are mine!" said Mr. Miller, very sharply. "How much shall I give you the day?"

"Auchty pund, sir, if you please—the lave when you like; I ken ye, Mr. Miller."

While counting her the notes, the purchaser said slyly to her:

"There's more than a hundred cran in the cutter, my woman."

"A little, sir," replied the vender; "but, ere I could count them till ye by baskets, they would lose seven or eight cran in book,* your gain, my loss."

*Bulk.

"You are a vara intelligent young person," said Mr. Miller, gravely.

"Ye had measured them wi' your walking-stick, sir; there's just ae scale ye didna wipe off, though ye are a carefu' mon, Mr. Miller; sae I laid the bait for ye an' fine ye took it."

Miller took out his snuff-box, and tapping it said:

"Will ye go into partnership with me, my dear?"

"Ay, sir!" was the reply. "When I'm aulder an' ye're younger."

At this moment the four merchants, believing it useless to disguise their co-operation, returned to see what could be done.

"We shall give you a guinea a barrel."

"Why, ye offered her twenty-two shillings before."

"That we never did, Mr. Miller."

"Haw! haw!" went Flucker.

Christie looked down and blushed.

Eyes met eyes, and without a word spoken all was comprehended and silently approved. There was no nonsense uttered
about morality in connection with dealing.

Mr. Miller took an enormous pinch of snuff, and drew for the
benefit of all present the following inference:

MR. MILLER'S APOTHEGM.

"Friends and neighbors! when a man's heed is gray with age
and thoucht *(pause)* he's just fit to go to schule to a young
lass o' twenty."

There was a certain middle-aged fishwife, called Beeny
Liston, a tenant of Christie Johnstone's; she had not paid her
rent for some time, and she had not been pressed for it;
whether this, or the whisky she was in the habit of taking,
rankled in her mind, certain it is she had always an ill word
for her landlady.

She now met her, envied her success, and called out in a
coarse tone:

"Oh, ye're a gallant quean; ye'll be waur than ever the noo."

"What's wrang, if ye please?" said the Johnstone, sharply.

Reader, did you ever see two fallow bucks commence a
duel?

They strut round, eight yards apart, tails up, look carefully
another way to make the other think it all means nothing,
and, being both equally sly, their horns come together as if
by concert.

Even so commenced this duel of tongues between these

Charles Reade

two heroines.

Beeny Liston, looking at everybody but Christie, addressed the natives who were congregating thus:

"Did ever ye hear o' a decent lass taking the herrin' oot o' the men's mooths?—is yon a woman's pairt, I'm asking ye?"

On this, Christie, looking carefully at all the others except Beeny, inquired with an air of simple curiosity:

"Can onybody tell me wha Liston Carnie's drunken wife is speakin' till? no to ony decent lass, though. Na! ye ken she wad na hae th' impudence!"

"Oh, ye ken fine I'm speakin' till yoursel'."

Here the horns clashed together.

"To me, woman?" *(with admirably acted surprise.)* "Oo, ay! it will be for the twa years' rent you're awin me. Giest!"

Beeny Liston. "Ye're just the impudentest girrl i' the toon, an' ye hae proved it the day" (her arms akimbo).

Christie (arms akimbo). "Me, impudent? how daur ye speak against my charackter, that's kenned for decency o' baith sides the Firrth."

Beeny (contemptuously). "Oh, ye're sly enough to beguile the men, but we ken ye."

Christie. "I'm no sly, and" *(drawing near and hissing the words)* "I'm no like the woman Jean an' I saw in Rose Street, dead drunk on the causeway, while her mon was working for her at sea. If ye're no ben your hoose in ae minute, I'll say that will gar Liston Carnie fling ye ower the pier-head, ye fool-moothed drunken leear—Scairt!"*

*A local word; a corruption from the French *Sortez.*

If my reader has seen and heard Mademoiselle Rachel utter her famous *Sortez,* in "Virginie," he knows exactly with what a gesture and tone the Johnstone uttered this word.

Beeny (in a voice of whining surprise). "Hech! what a spite Flucker Johnstone's dochter has taen against us."

Christie. "Scairt!"

Beeny (in a coaxing voice, and moving a step). "Aweel! what's a' your paession, my boenny woman?"

Christie. "Scairt!"

Beeny retired before the thunder and lightning of indignant virtue.

Then all the fishboys struck up a dismal chant of victory.

"Yoo-hoo—Custy's won the day—Beeny's scair*tit,"* going up on the last syllable.

Christie moved slowly away toward her own house, but before she could reach the door she began to whimper—little fool.

Thereat chorus of young Athenians chanted:

"Yu-hoo! come back, Beeny, ye'll maybe win yet. Custy's away gree*tin" (going up on the last syllable).*

"I'm no greetin, ye rude bairns," said Christie, bursting into tears, and retiring as soon as she had effected that proof of her philosophy.

It was about four hours later; Christie had snatched some repose. The wind, as Flucker prognosticated, had grown into a very heavy gale, and the Firth was brown and boiling.

Suddenly a clamor was heard on the shore, and soon after a fishwife made her appearance, with rather a singular burden.

Her husband, ladies; *rien que cela.*

She had him by the scruff of the neck; he was *dos-'a-dos,* with his booted legs kicking in the air, and his fists making warlike but idle demonstrations and his mouth uttering ineffectual bad language.

This worthy had been called a coward by Sandy Liston, and being about to fight with him, and get thrashed, his wife had whipped him up and carried him away; she now flung him down, at some risk of his equilibrium.

"Ye are not fit to feicht wi' Sandy Liston," said she; "if ye are for feichtin, here's for ye."

As a comment to this proposal, she tucked up the sleeves of her short gown. He tried to run by her; she caught him by the bosom, and gave him a violent push, that sent him several paces backward; he looked half fierce, half astounded; ere he could quite recover himself, his little servant forced a pipe into his hand, and he smoked contented and peaceable.

Before tobacco the evil passions fall, they tell me.

The cause of this quarrel soon explained itself; up came

Sandy Liston, cursing and swearing.

"What! ye hae gotten till your wife's; that's the place for ye; to say there's a brig in distress, and ye'll let her go on the rocks under your noses. But what are ye afraid o'? there's na danger?"

"Nae danger!" said one of the reproached, "are ye fou?"

"Ye are fou wi' fear yoursel'; of a' the beasts that crawl the airth, a cooward is the ugliest, I think."

"The wifes will no let us," said one, sulkily.

"It's the woman in your hairts that keeps ye," roared Sandy hoarsely; "curse ye, ye are sure to dee ane day, and ye are sure to be—!" (a past participle) "soon or late, what signifies when? Oh! curse the hour ever I was born amang sic a cooardly crew." *(Gun at sea.)*

"There!"

"She speaks till ye, hersel'; she cries for maircy; to think that, of a' that hear ye cry, Alexander Liston is the only mon mon enough to answer." *(Gun.)*

"You are mistaken, Mr. Alexander Liston," said a clear, smart voice, whose owner had mingled unobserved with the throng; "there are always men to answer such occasions; now, my lads, your boats have plenty of beam, and, well handled, should live in any sea; who volunteers with Alexander Liston and me?"

The speaker was Lord Ipsden.

The fishwives of Newhaven, more accustomed to measure

men than poor little Lady Barbara Sinclair, saw in this man what in point of fact he was—a cool, daring devil, than whom none more likely to lead men into mortal danger, or pull them through it, for that matter.

They recognized their natural enemy, and collected together against him, like hens at the sight of a hawk.

"And would you really entice our men till their death?"

"My life's worth as much as theirs, I suppose.

"Nae! your life! it's na worth a button; when you dee, your next kin will dance, and wha'll greet? but our men hae wife and bairns to look till." *(Gun at sea.)*

"Ah! I didn't look at it in that light," said Lord Ipsden. He then demanded paper and ink; Christie Johnstone, who had come out of her house, supplied it from her treasures, and this cool hand actually began to convey a hundred and fifty thousand pounds away, upon a sheet of paper blowing in the wind; when he had named his residuary legatee, and disposed of certain large bequests, he came to the point—

"Christie Johnstone, what can these people live on? two hundred a year? living is cheap here—confound the wind!"

"Twahundred? Fifty! Vile count."

"Don't call me vile count. I am Ipsden, and my name's Richard. Now, then, be smart with your names."

Three men stepped forward, gave their names, had their widows provided for, and went for their sou'westers, etc.

"Stay," said Lord Ipsden, writing. "To Christina Johnstone,

out of respect for her character, one thousand pounds."

"Richard! dinna gang," cried Christie, "oh, dinna gang, dinna gang, dinna gang; it's no your business."

"Will you lend me your papa's Flushing jacket and sou'wester, my dear? If I was sure to be drowned, I'd go!"

Christie ran in for them.

In the mean time, discomposed by the wind, and by feelings whose existence neither he, nor I, nor any one suspected, Saunders, after a sore struggle between the frail man and the perfect domestic, blurted out:

"My lord, I beg your lordship's pardon, but it blows tempestuous."

"That is why the brig wants us," was the reply.

"My lord, I beg your lordship's pardon," whimpered Saunders. "But, oh! my lord, don't go; it's all very well for fishermen to be drowned; it is their business, but not yours, my lord."

"Saunders, help me on with this coat."

Christie had brought it.

"Yes, my lord," said Saunders, briskly, his second nature reviving.

His lordship, while putting on the coat and hat, undertook to cool Mr. Saunders's aristocratic prejudices.

"Should Alexander Liston and I be drowned," said he,

coolly, "when our bones come ashore, you will not know which are the fisherman's and which the viscount's." So saying, he joined the enterprise.

"I shall pray for ye, lad," said Christie Johnstone, and she retired for that purpose.

Saunders, with a heavy heart, to the nearest tavern, to prepare an account of what he called "Heroism in High Life," large letters, and the usual signs of great astonishment!!!!! for the *Polytechnic Magazine.*

The commander of the distressed vessel had been penny-wise. He had declined a pilot off the Isle of May, trusting to fall in with one close to the port of Leith; but a heavy gale and fog had come on; he knew himself in the vicinity of dangerous rocks; and, to make matters worse, his ship, old and sore battered by a long and stormy voyage, was leaky; and unless a pilot came alongside, his fate would be, either to founder, or run upon the rocks, where he must expect to go to pieces in a quarter of an hour.

The Newhaven boat lay in comparatively smooth water, on the lee side of the pier.

Our adventurers got into her, stepped the mast, set a small sail, and ran out! Sandy Liston held the sheet, passed once round the belaying-pin, and whenever a larger wave than usual came at them, he slacked the sheet, and the boat, losing her way, rose gently, like a cork, upon seas that had seemed about to swallow her.

But seen from the shore it was enough to make the most experienced wince; so completely was this wooden shell lost to sight, as she descended from a wave, that each time her reappearance seemed a return from the dead.

The weather was misty—the boat was soon lost sight of; the story remains ashore.

Charles Reade

CHAPTER XIV

IT was an hour later; the natives of the New Town had left the pier, and were about their own doors, when three Buckhaven fishermen came slowly up from the pier; these men had arrived in one of their large fishing-boats, which defy all weather.

The men came slowly up; their petticoat trousers were drenched, and their neck-handkerchiefs and hair were wet with spray.

At the foot of the New Town they stood still and whispered to each other.

There was something about these men that drew the eye of Newhaven upon them.

In the first place a Buckhaven man rarely communicates with natives of Newhaven, except at the pier, where he brings in his cod and ling from the deep sea, flings them out like stones, and sells them to the fishwives; then up sail and away for Fifeshire.

But these men evidently came ashore to speak to some one in the town.

They whispered together; something appeared to be proposed and demurred to; but at last two went slowly back toward the pier, and the eldest remained, with a fisherman's long mackintosh coat in his hand which the others had given him as they left him.

With this in his hand, the Buckhaven fisherman stood in an irresolute posture; he looked down, and seemed to ask himself what course he should take.

"What's wrang?" said Jean Carnie, who, with her neighbors, had observed the men; "I wish yon man may na hae ill news."

"What ill news wad he hae?" replied another.

"Are ony freends of Liston Carnie here?" said the fisherman.

"The wife's awa' to Granton, Beeny Liston they ca' her— there's his house," added Jean, pointing up the row.

"Ay," said the fisherman, "I ken he lived there."

"Lived there!" cried Christie Johnstone. "Oh, what's this?"

"Freends," said the man, gravely, "his boat is driving keel uppermost in Kircauldy Bay. We passed her near enough to read the name upon her."

"But the men will have won to shore, please God?"

The fisherman shook his head.

"She'll hae coupit a mile wast Inch Keith, an' the tide rinning aff the island an' a heavy sea gaun. This is a' Newhaven we'll see of them *(holding up the coat)* "till they rise to the top in three weeks' time."

The man then took the coat, which was now seen to be drenched with water, and hung it up on a line not very far from its unfortunate owner's house. Then, in the same grave and subdued tone in which he had spoken all along, he said, "We are sorry to bring siccan a tale into your toon," and slowly moved off to rejoin his comrades, who had waited for him at no great distance. They then passed through the Old Town, and in five minutes the calamity was known to the whole place.

After the first stupor, the people in the New Town collected into knots, and lamented their hazardous calling, and feared for the lives of those that had just put to sea in this fatal gale for the rescue of strangers, and the older ones failed not to match this present sorrow with others within their recollection.

In the middle of this, Flucker Johnstone came hastily in from the Old Town and told them he had seen the wife, Beeny Liston, coming through from Granton.

The sympathy of all was instantly turned in this direction.

"She would hear the news."

"It would fall on her like a thunderclap."

"What would become of her?"

Every eye was strained toward the Old Town, and soon the poor woman was seen about to emerge from it; but she was walking in her usual way, and they felt she could not carry her person so if she knew.

At the last house she was seen to stop and speak to a fisherman and his wife that stood at their own door.

"They are telling her," was then the cry.

Beeny Liston then proceeded on her way.

Every eye was strained.

No! they had not told her.

She came gayly on, the unconscious object of every eye and every heart.

The hands of this people were hard, and their tongues rude, but they shrunk from telling this poor woman of her bereavement—they thought it kinder she should know it under her own roof, from her friends or neighbors, than from comparative strangers.

She drew near her own door.

And now a knot collected round Christie Johnstone, and urged her to undertake the sad task.

"You that speak sa learned, Christie, ye should tell her; we daur na."

"How can I tell her?" said Christie, turning pale. "How will I tell her? I'se try."

She took one trembling step to meet the woman.

Beeny's eye fell upon her.

"Ay! here's the Queen o' Newhaven," cried she, in a loud and rather coarse voice. "The men will hae ta leave the place now y' are turned fisherman, I daur say."

"Oh, dinna fieicht on me! dinna fieicht on me!" cried Christie, trembling.

"Maircy on us," said the other, "auld Flucker Johnstone's dochter turned humble. What next?"

"I'm vexed for speaking back till ye the morn," faltered Christie.

"Hett," said the woman carelessly, "let yon flea stick i' the wa'. I fancy I began on ye. Aweel, Cirsty," said she, falling into a friendlier tone; "it's the place we live in spoils us— Newhaven's an impudent toon, as sure as deeth.

"I passed through the Auld Toon the noo—a place I never speak in; an' if they did na glower at me as I had been a strange beast.

"They cam' to their very doors to glower at me; if ye'll believe me, I thoucht shame.

"At the hinder end my paassion got up, and I faced a wife East-by, and I said, 'What gars ye glower at me that way, ye ignorant woman?' ye would na think it, she answered like honey itsel'. 'I'm askin' your paarrdon,' says she; and her mon by her side said, 'Gang hame to your ain hoose, my woman, and Gude help ye, and help us a' at our need,' the decent mon. 'It's just there I'm for,' said I, 'to get my mon his breakfast.'"

All who heard her drew their breath with difficulty.

The woman then made for her own house, but in going up

the street she passed the wet coat hanging on the line.

She stopped directly.

They all trembled—they had forgotten the coat—it was all over; the coat would tell the tale.

"Aweel," said she, "I could sweer that's Liston Carnie's coat, a droukit wi' the rain; then she looked again at it, and added, slowly, "if I did na ken he has his away wi' him at the piloting." And in another moment she was in her own house, leaving them all standing there half stupefied.

Christie had indeed endeavored to speak, but her tongue had cloven to her mouth.

While they stood looking at one another, and at Beeny Liston's door, a voice that seemed incredibly rough, loud and harsh, jarred upon them; it was Sandy Liston, who came in from Leith, shouting:

"Fifty pounds for salvage, lasses! is na thaat better than staying cooard-like aside the women?"

"Whisht! whisht!" cried Christie.

"We are in heavy sorrow; puir Liston Cairnie and his son Willy lie deed at the bottom o' the Firrth."

"Gude help us!" said Sandy, and his voice sank.

"An', oh, Sandy, the wife does na ken, and it's hairt-breaking to see her, and hear her; we canna get her tell't; ye're the auldest mon here; ye'll tell her, will ye no, Sandy?"

"No, me, that' I will not!"

"Oh, yes; ye are kenned for your stoot heart, an' courage; ye come fra' facing the sea an' wind in a bit yawl."

"The sea and the wind," cried he, contemptuously; "they be —, I'm used wi' them; but to look a woman i' the face, an' tell her her mon and her son are drowned since yestreen, I hae na coorage for that."

All further debate was cut short by the entrance of one who came expressly to discharge the sad duty all had found so difficult. It was the Presbyterian clergyman of the place; he waved them back. "I know, I know," said he, solemnly. "Where is the wife?"

She came out of her house at this moment, as it happened, to purchase something at Drysale's shop, which was opposite.

"Beeny," said the clergyman, "I have sorrowful tidings."

"Tell me them, sir," said she, unmoved. "Is it a deeth?" added she, quietly.

"It is!—death, sudden and terrible; in your own house I must tell it you—(and may God show me how to break it to her)."

He entered her house.

"Aweel," said the woman to the others, "it maun be some far-awa cousin, or the like, for Liston an' me hae nae near freends. Meg, ye idle fuzzy," screamed she to her servant, who was one of the spectators, "your pat is no on yet; div ye think the men will no be hungry when they come in fra' the sea?"

"They will never hunger nor thirst ony mair," said Jean, solemnly, as the bereaved woman entered her own door.

There ensued a listless and fearful silence.

Every moment some sign of bitter sorrow was expected to break forth from the house, but none came; and amid the expectation and silence the waves dashed louder and louder, as it seemed, against the dike, conscious of what they had done.

At last, in a moment, a cry of agony arose, so terrible that all who heard it trembled, and more than one woman shrieked in return, and fled from the door, at which, the next moment, the clergyman stood alone, collected, but pale, and beckoned. Several women advanced.

"One woman," said he.

Jean Carnie was admitted; and after a while returned.

"She is come to hersel'," whispered she; "I am no weel mysel'." And she passed into her own house.

Then Flucker crept to the door to see.

"Oh, dinna spy on her," cried Christie.

"Oh, yes, Flucker," said many voices.

"He is kneelin'," said Flucker. "He has her hand, to gar her kneel tae—she winna—she does na see him, nor hear him; he will hae her. He has won her to kneel—he is prayin, an' greetin aside her. I canna see noo, my een's blinded."

"He's a gude mon," said Christie. "Oh, what wad we do without the ministers?"

Sandy Liston had been leaning sorrowfully against the wall

of the next house; he now broke out:

"An auld shipmate at the whale-fishing!!! an' noow we'll never lift the dredging sang thegither again, in yon dirty detch that's droowned him; I maun hae whisky, an' forget it a'."

He made for the spirit-shop like a madman; but ere he could reach the door a hand was laid on him like a vise. Christie Johnstone had literally sprung on him. She hated this horrible vice—had often checked him; and now it seemed so awful a moment for such a sin, that she forgot the wild and savage nature of the man, who had struck his own sister, and seriously hurt her, a month before—she saw nothing but the vice and its victim, and she seized him by the collar, with a grasp from which he in vain attempted to shake himself loose.

"No! ye'll no gang there at siccan a time."

"Hands off, ye daft jaud," roared he, "or there'll be another deeth i' the toon."

At the noise Jean Carnie ran in.

"Let the ruffian go," cried she, in dismay. "Oh, Christie, dinna put your hand on a lion's mane."

"Yes, I'll put my hand on his mane, ere I'll let him mak a beast o' himsel'."

"Sandy, if ye hurt her, I'll find twenty lads that will lay ye deed at her feet."

"Haud your whisht," said Christie, very sharply, "he's no to be threetened."

Sandy Liston, black and white with rage, ground his teeth together, and said, lifting his hand, "Wull ye let me go, or must I tak my hand till ye?"

"No!" said Christie, "I'll no let ye go, *sae look me i' the face; Flucker's dochter, your auld comrade, that saved your life at Holy Isle, think o' his face—an' look in mines—an' strike me!!!"*

They glared on one another—he fiercely and unsteadily; she firmly and proudly.

Jean Carnie said afterward, "Her eyes were like coals of fire."

"Ye are doing what nae mon i' the toon daur; ye are a bauld, unwise lassy."

"It's you mak me bauld," was the instant reply. "I saw ye face the mad sea, to save a ship fra' the rocks, an' will I fear a mon's hand, when I can save" *(rising to double her height)* "my feyther's auld freend fra' the puir mon's enemy, the enemy o' mankind, the cursed, cursed drink? Oh, Sandy Liston, hoow could ye think to put an enemy in your mooth to steal awa your brains!"

"This 's no Newhaven chat; wha lairns ye sic words o' power?"

"A deed mon!"

"I would na wonder, y' are no canny; she's ta'en a' the poower oot o' my body, I think." Then suddenly descending to a tone of abject submission, "What's your pleesure, Flucker Johnstone's dochter?"

She instantly withdrew the offending grasp, and, leaning affectionately on his shoulder, she melted into her rich Ionic tones.

"It's no a time for sin; ye'll sit by my fire, an' get your dinner; a bonny haggis hae I for you an' Flucker, an' we'll improve this sorrowfu' judgment; an' ye'll tell me o' auld times—o' my feyther dear, that likeit ye weel, Sandy—o' the storrms ye hae weathered, side by side—o' the muckle whales ye killed Greenland way—an' abune a', o' the lives ye hae saved at sea, by your daurin an' your skell; an', oh, Sandy, will na that be better as sit an' poor leequid damnation doown your throat, an' gie awa the sense an' feeling o' a mon for a sair heed and an ill name?"

"I'se gang, my lamb," said the rough man, quite subdued; "I daur say whisky will no pass my teeth the day."

And so he went quietly away, and sat by Christie's fireside.

Jean and Christie went toward the boats.

Jean, after taking it philosophically for half a minute, began to whimper.

"What's wrang?" said Christie.

"Div ye think my hairt's no in my mooth wi' you gripping yon fierce robber?"

Here a young fishwife, with a box in her hand, who had followed them, pulled Jean by the coats.

"Hets," said Jean, pulling herself free.

The child then, with a pertinacity these little animals have, pulled Christie's coats.

"Hets," said Christie, freeing herself more gently.

"Ye suld mairry Van Amburgh," continued Jean; "ye are just such a lass as he is a lad."

Christie smiled proudly, was silent, but did not disown the comparison.

The little fishwife, unable to attract attention by pulling, opened her box, and saying, "Lasses, I'll let ye see my presoner. Hech! he's boenny!" pulled out a mouse by a string fastened to his tail and set him in the midst for friendly admiration.

"I dinna like it—I dinna like it!" screamed Christie. "Jean, put it away—it fears me, Jean!" This she uttered (her eyes almost starting from her head with unaffected terror) at the distance of about eight yards, whither she had arrived in two bounds that would have done no discredit to an antelope.

"Het," said Jean, uneasily, "hae ye coowed you savage, to be scared at the wee beastie?"

Christie, looking askant at the animal, explained: "A moose is an awesome beast—it's no like a mon!" and still her eye was fixed by fascination upon the four-footed danger.

Jean, who had not been herself in genuine tranquillity, now turned savagely on the little Wombwelless. "An' div ye really think ye are to come here wi' a' the beasts i' the Airk? Come, awa ye go, the pair o' ye."

These severe words, and a smart push, sent the poor little biped off roaring, with the string over her shoulder, recklessly dragging the terrific quadruped, which made fruitless grabs at the shingle.—*Moral.* Don't terrify bigger folk than yourself.

Christie had intended to go up to Edinburgh with her eighty pounds, but there was more trouble in store this eventful day.

Flucker went out after dinner, and left her with Sandy Liston, who was in the middle of a yarn, when some one came running in and told her Flucker was at the pier crying for her. She inquired what was the matter. "Come, an' ye'll see," was all the answer. She ran down to the pier. There was poor Flucker lying on his back; he had slipped from the pier into a boat that lay alongside; the fall was considerable; for a minute he had been insensible, then he had been dreadfully sick, and now he was beginning to feel his hurt; he was in great anguish; nobody knew the extent of his injuries; he would let nobody touch him; all his cry was for his sister. At last she came; they all made way for her; he was crying for her as she came up.

"My bairn! my bairn!" cried she, and the poor little fellow smiled, and tried to raise himself toward her.

She lifted him gently in her arms—she was powerful, and affection made her stronger; she carried him in her arms all the way home, and laid him on her own bed. Willy Liston, her discarded suitor, ran for the surgeon. There were no bones broken, but his ankle was severely sprained, and he had a terrible bruise on the loins; his dark, ruddy face was streaked and pale; but he never complained after he found himself at home.

Christie hovered round him, a ministering angel, applying to him with a light and loving hand whatever could ease his pain; and he watched her with an expression she had never noticed in his eye before.

At last, after two hours' silence, he made her sit in full view, and then he spoke to her; and what think you was the subject of his discourse?

He turned to and told her, one after another, without preface, all the loving things she had done to him ever since he was five years old. Poor boy, he had never shown much gratitude, but he had forgotten nothing, literally nothing.

Christie was quite overcome with this unexpected trait; she drew him gently to her bosom, and wept over him; and it was sweet to see a brother and sister treat each other almost like lovers, as these two began to do—they watched each other's eye so tenderly.

This new care kept the sister in her own house all the next day; but toward the evening Jean, who knew her other anxiety, slipped in and offered to take her place for an hour by Flucker's side; at the same time she looked one of those signals which are too subtle for any but woman to understand.

Christie drew her aside, and learned that Gatty and his mother were just coming through from Leith; Christie ran for her eighty pounds, placed them in her bosom, cast a hasty glance at a looking-glass, little larger than an oyster-shell, and ran out.

"Hech! What pleased the auld wife will be to see he has a lass that can mak auchty pund in a morning."

This was Christie's notion.

At sight of them she took out the banknotes, and with eyes

glistening and cheeks flushing she cried:

"Oh, Chairles, ye'll no gang to jail—I hae the siller!" and she offered him the money with both hands, and a look of tenderness and modesty that embellished human nature.

Ere he could speak, his mother put out her hand, and not rudely, but very coldly, repelling Christie's arm, said in a freezing manner:

"We are much obliged to you, but my son's own talents have rescued him from his little embarrassment."

"A nobleman has bought my picture," said Gatty, proudly.

"For one hundred and fifty pounds," said the old lady, meaning to mark the contrast between that sum and what Christie had in her hand.

Christie remained like a statue, with her arms extended, and the bank-notes in her hand; her features worked—she had much ado not to cry; and any one that had known the whole story, and seen this unmerited repulse, would have felt for her; but her love came to her aid, she put the notes in her bosom, sighed and said:

"I would hae likeit to hae been the first, ye ken, but I'm real pleased."

"But, mother," said Gatty, "it was very kind of Christie all the same. Oh, Christie!" said he, in a tone of despair.

At this kind word Christie's fortitude was sore tried; she turned away her head; she was far too delicate to let them know who had sent Lord Ipsden to buy the picture.

While she turned away, Mrs. Gatty said in her son's ear:

"Now, I have your solemn promise to do it here, and at once; you will find me on the beach behind these boats—do it."

The reader will understand that during the last few days Mrs. Gatty had improved her advantage, and that Charles had positively consented to obey her; the poor boy was worn out with the struggle—he felt he must have peace or die; he was thin and pale, and sudden twitches came over him; his temperament was not fit for such a battle; and, it is to be observed, nearly all the talk was on one side. He had made one expiring struggle—he described to his mother an artist's nature; his strength, his weakness—he besought her not to be a slave to general rules, but to inquire what sort of a companion the individual Gatty needed; he lashed with true but brilliant satire the sort of wife his mother was ready to see him saddled with—a stupid, unsympathizing creature, whose ten children would, by nature's law, be also stupid, and so be a weight on him till his dying day. He painted Christie Johnstone, mind and body, in words as true and bright as his colors; he showed his own weak points, her strong ones, and how the latter would fortify the former.

He displayed, in short, in one minute, more intellect than his mother had exhibited in sixty years; and that done, with all his understanding, wit and eloquence, he succumbed like a child to her stronger will—he promised to break with Christie Johnstone.

When Christie had recovered her composure and turned round to her companions, she found herself alone with Charles.

"Chairles," said she, gravely.

"Christie," said he, uneasily.

"Your mother does na like me. Oh, ye need na deny it; and we are na together as we used to be, my lad."

"She is prejudiced; but she has been the best of mothers to me, Christie."

"Aweel."

"Circumstances compel me to return to England."

(Ah, coward! anything but the real truth!)

"Aweel, Chairles, it will no be for lang."

"I don't know; you will not be so unhappy as I shall—at least I hope not."

"Hoow do ye ken that?"

"Christie, do you remember the first night we danced together?"

"Ay."

"And we walked in the cool by the seaside, and I told you the names of the stars, and you said those were not their real names, but nicknames we give them here on earth. I loved you that first night."

"And I fancied you the first time I set eyes on you."

"How can I leave you, Christie? What shall I do?"

"I ken what I shall do," answered Christie coolly; then,

bursting into tears, she added, "I shall dee! I shall dee!"

"No! you must not say so; at least I will never love any one but you."

"An' I'll live as I am a' my days for your sake. Oh, England! I hae likeit ye sae weel, ye suld na rob me o' my lad—he's a' the joy I hae!"

"I love you," said Gatty. "Do you love me?"

All the answer was, her head upon his shoulder.

"I can't do it," thought Gatty, "and I won't! Christie," said he, "stay here, don't move from here." And he dashed among the boats in great agitation.

He found his mother rather near the scene of the late conference.

"Mother," said he, fiercely, like a coward as he was, "ask me no more, my mind is made up forever; I will not do this scoundrelly, heartless, beastly, ungrateful action you have been pushing me to so long."

"Take care, Charles, take care," said the old woman, trembling with passion, for this was a new tone for her son to take with her. "You had my blessing the other day, and you saw what followed it; do not tempt me to curse an undutiful, disobedient, ungrateful son."

"I must take my chance," said he, desperately, "for I am under a curse any way! I placed my ring on her finger, and held up my hand to God and swore she should be my wife; she has my ring and my oath, and I will not perjure myself even for my mother."

"Your ring! Not the ruby ring I gave you from your dead father's finger—not that! not that!"

"Yes! yes! I tell you yes! and if he was alive, and saw her, and knew her goodness, he would have pity on me, but I have no friend; you see how ill you have made me, but you have no pity; I could not have believed it; but, since you have no mercy on me, I will have the more mercy on myself; I marry her to-morrow, and put an end to all this shuffling and maneuvering against an angel! I am not worthy of her, but I'll marry her to-morrow. Good-by."

"Stay!" said the old woman, in a terrible voice; "before you destroy me and all I have lived for, and suffered, and pinched for, hear me; if that ring is not off the hussy's finger in half an hour, and you my son again, I fall on this sand and—"

"Then God have mercy upon me, for I'll see the whole creation lost eternally ere I'll wrong the only creature that is an ornament to the world."

He was desperate; and the weak, driven to desperation, are more furious than the strong.

It was by Heaven's mercy that neither mother nor son had time to speak again.

As they faced each other, with flaming eyes and faces, all self-command gone, about to utter hasty words, and lay up regret, perhaps for all their lives to come, in a moment, as if she had started from the earth, Christie Johnstone stood between them!

Gatty's words, and, still more, his hesitation, had made her quick intelligence suspect. She had resolved to know the truth; the boats offered every facility for listening—she had heard every word.

She stood between the mother and son.

They were confused, abashed, and the hot blood began to leave their faces.

She stood erect like a statue, her cheek pale as ashes, her eyes glittering like basilisks, she looked at neither of them.

She slowly raised her left hand, she withdrew a ruby ring from it, and dropped the ring on the sand between the two.

She turned on her heel, and was gone as she had come, without a word spoken.

They looked at one another, stupefied at first; after a considerable pause the stern old woman stooped, picked up the ring, and, in spite of a certain chill that the young woman's majestic sorrow had given her, said, placing it on her own finger, "This is for your wife!!!"

"It will be for my coffin, then," said her son, so coldly, so bitterly and so solemnly that the mother's heart began to quake.

"Mother," said he calmly, "forgive me, and accept your son's arm.

"I will, my son!"

"We are alone in the world now, mother."

Mrs. Gatty had triumphed, but she felt the price of her triumph more than her victory. It had been done in one moment, that for which she had so labored, and it seemed that had she spoken long ago to Christie, instead of Charles, it could have been done at any moment.

Strange to say, for some minutes the mother felt more uneasy than her son; she was a woman, after all, and could measure a woman's heart, and she saw how deep the wound she had given one she was now compelled to respect.

Charles, on the other hand, had been so harassed backward and forward, that to him certainty was relief; it was a great matter to be no longer called upon to decide. His mother had said, "Part," and now Christie had said, "Part"; at least the affair was taken out of his hands, and his first feeling was a heavenly calm.

In this state he continued for about a mile, and he spoke to his mother about his art, sole object now; but after the first mile he became silent, *distrait;* Christie's pale face, her mortified air, when her generous offer was coldly repulsed, filled him with remorse. Finally, unable to bear it, yet not daring to speak, he broke suddenly from his mother without a word, and ran wildly back to Newhaven; he looked back only once, and there stood his mother, pale, with her hands piteously lifted toward heaven.

By the time he got to Newhaven he was as sorry for her as for Christie. He ran to the house of the latter; Flucker and Jean told him she was on the beach. He ran to the beach! he did not see her at first, but, presently looking back, he saw her, at the edge of the boats, in company with a gentleman in a boating-dress. He looked—could he believe his eyes? he saw Christie Johnstone kiss this man's hand, who then, taking her head gently in his two hands, placed a kiss upon her brow, while she seemed to yield lovingly to the caress.

Gatty turned faint, sick; for a moment everything swam

before his eyes; he recovered himself, they were gone.

He darted round to intercept them; Christie had slipped away somewhere; he encountered the man alone!

Charles Reade

CHAPTER XV

CHRISTIE'S situation requires to be explained.

On leaving Gatty and his mother, she went to her own house. Flucker—who after looking upon her for years as an inconvenient appendage, except at dinnertime, had fallen in love with her in a manner that was half pathetic, half laughable, all things considered—saw by her face she had received a blow, and raising himself in the bed, inquired anxiously, "What ailed her?"

At these kind words, Christie Johnstone laid her cheek upon the pillow beside Flucker's and said:

"Oh, my laamb, be kind to your puir sister fra' this hoor, for she has naething i' the warld noo but yoursel'."

Flucker began to sob at this.

Christie could not cry; her heart was like a lump of lead in her bosom; but she put her arm round his neck, and at the sight of his sympathy she panted heavily, but could not shed a tear—she was sore stricken.

Presently Jean came in, and, as the poor girl's head ached as well as her heart, they forced her to go and sit in the air. She took her creepie and sat, and looked on the sea; but, whether she looked seaward or landward, all seemed unreal; not things, but hard pictures of things, some moving, some still. Life seemed ended—she had lost her love.

An hour she sat in this miserable trance; she was diverted into a better, because a somewhat less dangerous form of grief, by one of those trifling circumstances that often penetrate to the human heart when inaccessible to greater things.

Willy the fiddler and his brother came through the town, playing as they went, according to custom; their music floated past Christie's ears like some drowsy chime, until, all of a sudden, they struck up the old English air, "Speed the Plow."

Now it was to this tune Charles Gatty had danced with her their first dance the night they made acquaintance.

Christie listened, lifted up her hands, and crying:

"Oh, what will I do? what will I do?" burst into a passion of grief.

She put her apron over her head, and rocked herself, and sobbed bitterly.

She was in this situation when Lord Ipsden, who was prowling about, examining the proportions of the boats, discovered her.

"Some one in distress—that was all in his way."

"Madam!" said he.

She lifted up her head.

"It is Christie Johnstone. I'm so glad; that is, I'm sorry you are crying, but I'm glad I shall have the pleasure of relieving you;" and his lordship began to feel for a check-book.

"And div ye really think siller's a cure for every grief!" said Christie, bitterly.

"I don't know," said his lordship; "it has cured them all as yet."

"It will na cure me, then!" and she covered her head with her apron again.

"I am very sorry," said he; "tell me" *(whispering),* "what is it? poor little Christie!"

"Dinna speak to me; I think shame; ask Jean. Oh, Richard, I'll no be lang in this warld!!!"

"Ah!" said he, "I know too well what it is now; I know, by sad experience. But, Christie, money will cure it in your case, and it shall, too; only, instead of five pounds, we must put a thousand pounds or two to your banker's account, and then they will all see your beauty, and run after you."

"How daur ye even to me that I'm seekin a lad?" cried she, rising from her stool; "I would na care suppose there was na a lad in Britain." And off she flounced.

"Offended her by my gross want of tact," thought the viscount.

She crept back, and two velvet lips touched his hand. That was because she had spoken harshly to a friend.

"Oh, Richard," said she, despairingly, "I'll no be lang in this warld."

He was touched; and it was then he took her head and kissed her brow, and said: "This will never do. My child, go home and have a nice cry, and I will speak to Jean; and, rely upon me, I will not leave the neighborhood till I have arranged it all to your satisfaction."

And so she went—a little, a very little, comforted by his tone and words.

Now this was all very pretty; but then seen at a distance of fifty yards it looked very ugly; and Gatty, who had never before known jealousy, the strongest and worst of human passions, was ripe for anything.

He met Lord Ipsden, and said at once, in his wise, temperate way:

"Sir, you are a villain!"

Ipsden. *"Plait-il?"*

Gatty. "You are a villain!"

Ipsden. "How do you make that out?"

Gatty. "But, of course, you are not a coward, too."

Ipsden (ironically). "You surprise me with your moderation, sir."

Gatty. "Then you will waive your rank—you are a lord, I believe-and give me satisfaction."

Ipsden. "My rank, sir, such as it is, engages me to give a proper answer to proposals of this sort; I am at your orders."

Gatty. "A man of your character must often have been called to an account by your victims, so—so—" (hesitating) "perhaps you will tell me the proper course."

Ipsden. "*I* shall send a note to the castle, and the colonel will send me down somebody with a mustache; I shall pretend to remember mustache, mustache will pretend he remembers me; he will then communicate with your friend, and they will arrange it all for us."

Gatty. "And, perhaps, through your licentiousness, one or both of us will be killed."

Ipsden. "Yes! but we need not trouble our heads about that— the seconds undertake everything."

Gatty. "I have no pistols."

Ipsden. "If you will do me the honor to use one of mine, it shall be at your service."

Gatty. "Thank you."

Ipsden. "To-morrow morning?"

Gatty. "No. I have four days' painting to do on my picture, I can't die till it is finished; Friday morning."

Ipsden. "(He is mad.) I wish to ask you a question, you will excuse my curiosity. Have you any idea what we are agreeing to differ about?"

Gatty. "The question does you little credit, my lord; that is to add insult to wrong."

He went off hurriedly, leaving Lord Ipsden mystified.

He thought Christie Johnstone was somehow connected with it; but, conscious of no wrong, he felt little disposed to put up with any insult, especially from this boy, to whom he had been kind, he thought.

His lordship was, besides, one of those good, simple-minded creatures, educated abroad, who, when invited to fight, simply bow, and load two pistols, and get themselves called at six; instead of taking down tomes of casuistry and puzzling their poor brains to find out whether they are gamecocks or capons, and why.

As for Gatty, he hurried home in a fever of passion, begged his mother's pardon, and reproached himself for ever having disobeyed her on account of such a perfidious creature as Christie Johnstone.

He then told her what he had seen, as distance and imagination had presented it to him; to his surprise the old lady cut him short.

"Charles," said she, "there is no need to take the girl's character away; she has but one fault—she is not in the same class of life as you, and such marriages always lead to misery; but in other respects she is a worthy young woman— don't speak against her character, or you will make my flesh creep; you don't know what her character is to a woman, high or low."

By this moderation, perhaps she held him still faster.

Friday morning arrived. Gatty had, by hard work, finished his picture, collected his sketches from nature, which were numerous, left by memorandum everything to his mother, and was, or rather felt, as ready to die as live.

He had hardly spoken a word or eaten a meal these four days; his mother was in anxiety about him. He rose early, and went down to Leith; an hour later, his mother, finding him gone out, rose and went to seek him at Newhaven.

Meantime Flucker had entirely recovered, but his sister's color had left her cheeks. The boy swore vengeance against the cause of her distress.

On Friday morning, then, there paced on Leith Sands two figures.

One was Lord Ipsden.

The other seemed a military gentleman, who having swallowed the mess-room poker, and found it insufficient, had added the ramrods of his company.

The more his lordship reflected on Gatty, the less inclined he had felt to invite a satirical young dog from barracks to criticise such a *rencontre;* he had therefore ordered Saunders to get up as a field-marshal, or some such trifle, and what Saunders would have called incomparable verticality was the result.

The painter was also in sight.

While he was coming up, Lord Ipsden was lecturing Marshal Saunders on a point on which that worthy had always thought himself very superior to his master—"Gentlemanly deportment."

"Now, Saunders, mind and behave like a gentleman, or we shall be found out."

"I trust, my lord, my conduct—"

"What I mean is, you must not be so overpoweringly gentleman-like as you are apt to be; no gentleman is so gentleman as all that; it could not be borne, *c'est suffoquant;* and a white handkerchief is unsoldier-like, and nobody ties a white handkerchief so well as that; of all the vices, perfection is the most intolerable." His lordship then touched with his cane the generalissimo's tie, whose countenance straightway fell, as though he had lost three successive battles.

Gatty came up.

They saluted.

"Where is your second, sir?" said the mare'chal.

"My second?" said Gatty. "Ah! I forgot to wake him—does it matter?"

"It is merely a custom," said Lord Ipsden, with a very slightly satirical manner. "Savanadero," said he, "do us the honor to measure the ground, and be everybody's second."

Savanadero measured the ground, and handed a pistol to each combatant, and struck an imposing attitude apart.

"Are you ready, gentlemen?" said this Jack-o'-both-sides.

"Yes!" said both.

Just as the signal was about to be given, an interruption occurred. "I beg your pardon, sir," said Lord Ipsden to his antagonist; "I am going to take a *liberty—a great liberty* with you, but I think you will find your pistol is only at half cock."

"Thank you, my lord; what am I to do with the thing?"

"Draw back the cock so, and be ready to fire?"

"So?" *Bang!*

He had touched the trigger as well as the cock, so off went the barker; and after a considerable pause the field-marshal sprang yelling into the air.

"Hallo!" cried Mr. Gatty.

"Ah! oh! I'm a dead man," whined the general.

"Nonsense!" said Ipsden, after a moment of anxiety. "Give yourself no concern, sir," said he, soothingly, to his antagonist—"a mere accident. Mare'chal, reload Mr. Gatty's pistol."

"Excuse me, my lord—"

"Load his pistol directly," said his lordship, sternly; "and behave like a gentleman."

"My lord! my lord! but where shall I stand to be safe?"

"Behind me!"

The commander of division advanced reluctantly for Gatty's pistol.

"No, my lord!" said Gatty, "it is plain I am not a fit

antagonist; I shall but expose myself—and my mother has separated us; I have lost her—if you do not win her some worse man may; but, oh! if you are a man, use her tenderly."

"Whom?"

"Christie Johnstone! Oh, sir, do not make her regret me too much! She was my treasure, my consolation—she was to be my wife, she would have cheered the road of life—it is a desert now. I loved her—I—I—"

Here the poor fellow choked.

Lord Ipsden turned round, and threw his pistol to Saunders, saying, "Catch that, Saunders."

Saunders, on the contrary, by a single motion changed his person from a vertical straight line to a horizontal line exactly parallel with the earth's surface, and the weapon sang innoxious over him.

His lordship then, with a noble defiance of etiquette, walked up to his antagonist and gave him his hand, with a motion no one could resist; for he felt for the poor fellow.

"It is all a mistake," said he. "There is no sentiment between La Johnstone and me but mutual esteem. I will explain the whole thing. *I* admire *her* for her virtue, her wit, her innocence, her goodness and all that sort of thing; and *she,* what *she* sees in *me,* I am sure I don't know," added he, slightly shrugging his aristocratic shoulders. "Do me the honor to breakfast with me at Newhaven."

"I have ordered twelve sorts of fish at the 'Peacock,' my lord," said Saunders.

Charles Reade

"Divine! (I hate fish) I told Saunders all would be hungry and none shot; by the by, you are winged, I think you said, Saunders?"

"No, my lord! but look at my trousers."

The bullet had cut his pantaloons.

"I see—only barked; so go and see about our breakfast."

"Yes, my lord" *(faintly)*.

"And draw on me for fifty pounds' worth of—new trousers."

Yes, my lord" *(sonorously)*.

The duelists separated, Gatty taking the short cut to Newhaven; he proposed to take his favorite swim there, to refresh himself before breakfast; and he went from his lordship a little cheered by remarks which fell from him, and which, though vague, sounded friendly—poor fellow, except when he had a brush in hand he was a dreamer.

This viscount, who did not seem to trouble his head about class dignity, was to convert his mother from her aristocratic tendencies or something.

Que sais-je? what will not a dreamer hope?

Lord Ipsden strolled along the sands, and judge his surprise, when, attended by two footmen, he met at that time in the morning Lady Barbara Sinclair

Lord Ipsden had been so disheartened and piqued by this lady's conduct that for a whole week he had not been near her. This line of behavior sometimes answers.

She met him with a grand display of cordiality.

She inquired, "Whether he had heard of a most gallant action, that, coupled with another circumstance" *(here she smiled),* "had in part reconciled her to the age we live in?"

He asked for further particulars.

She then informed him "that a ship had been ashore on the rocks, that no fisherman dared venture out, that a young gentleman had given them his whole fortune, and so bribed them to accompany him; that he had saved the ship and the men's lives, paid away his fortune, and lighted an odious cigar and gone home, never minding, amid the blessings and acclamations of a maritime population."

A beautiful story she told him; so beautiful, in fact, that until she had discoursed ten minutes he hardly recognized his own feat; but when he did he blushed inside as well as out with pleasure. Oh! music of music—praise from eloquent lips, and those lips the lips we love.

The next moment he felt ashamed; ashamed that Lady Barbara should praise him beyond his merits, as he conceived.

He made a faint hypocritical endeavor to moderate her eulogium; this gave matters an unexpected turn, Lady Barbara's eyes flashed defiance.

"I say it was a noble action, that one nursed in effeminacy (as you all are) should teach the hardy seamen to mock at peril—noble fellow!"

"He did a man's duty, Barbara."

"Ipsden, take care, you will make me hate you, if you detract from a deed you cannot emulate. This gentleman risked his own life to save others—he is a hero! I should know him by his face the moment I saw him. Oh, that I were such a man, or knew where to find such a creature!"

The water came into Lord Ipsden's eyes; he did not know what to say or do; he turned away his head. Lady Barbara was surprised; her conscience smote her.

"Oh, dear," said she, "there now, I have given you pain—forgive me; we can't all be heroes; dear Ipsden, don't think I despise you now as I used. Oh, no! I have heard of your goodness to the poor, and I have more experience now. There is nobody I esteem more than you, Richard, so you need not look so."

"Thank you, dearest Barbara."

"Yes, and if you were to be such a goose as to write me another letter proposing absurdities to me—"

"Would the answer be different?"

"Very different."

"Oh, Barbara, would you accept?"

"Why, of course not; but I would refuse civilly!"

"Ah!"

"There, don't sigh; I hate a sighing man. I'll tell you some-thing that I know will make you laugh." She then smiled saucily in his face, and said, "Do you remember Mr.—?"

L'effronte'e! this was the earnest man. But Ipsden was a match for her this time. "I think I do," said he; "a gentleman who wants to make John Bull little again into John Calf; but it won't do."

Her ladyship laughed. "Why did you not tell us that on Inch Coombe?"

"Because I had not read *The Catspaw* then."

"The Catspaw? Ah! I thought it could not be you. Whose is it?"

"Mr. Jerrold's."

"Then Mr. Jerrold is cleverer than you."

"It is possible."

"It is certain! Well, Mr. Jerrold and Lord Ipsden, you will both be glad to hear that it was, in point of fact, a bull that confuted the advocate of the Middle Ages; we were walking; he was telling me manhood was extinct except in a few earnest men who lived upon the past, its associations, its truth; when a horrid bull gave—oh—such a bellow! and came trotting up. I screamed and ran—I remember nothing but arriving at the stile, and lo, on the other side, offering me his arm with *empressment* across the wooden barrier was—"

"Well?"

"Well! don't you see?"

"No—oh—yes, I see!—fancy—ah! Shall I tell you how he came to get first over? He ran more earnestly than you."

'It is not Mr. Jerrold this time, I presume," said her satirical ladyship.

"No! you cannot always have him. I venture to predict your ladyship on your return home gave this mediaeval personage his *conge'.*"

"No!"

"No?"

"I gave it him at the stile! Let us be serious, if you please; I have a confidence to make you, Ipsden. Frankly, I owe you some apology for my conduct of late; I meant to be reserved —I have been rude—but you shall judge me. A year ago you made me some proposals; I rejected them because, though I like you—"

"You like me?"

"I detest your character. Since then, my West India estate has been turned into specie; that specie, the bulk of my fortune, placed on board a vessel; that vessel lost, at least we think so—she has not been heard of."

"My dear cousin."

"Do you comprehend that now I am cooler than ever to all young gentlemen who have large incomes, and" (holding out her hand like an angel) "I must trouble you to forgive me."

He kissed her lovely hand.

"I esteem you more and more," said he. "You ought, for it has been a hard struggle to me not to adore you, because you are so improved, *mon cousin.*"

"Is it possible? In what respect?"

"You are browner and charitabler; and I should have been very kind to you—mawkishly kind, I fear, my sweet cousin, if this wretched money had not gone down in the *Tisbe.*"

"Hallo!" cried the viscount.

"Ah!" squeaked Lady Barbara, unused to such interjections.

"Gone down in what?" said Ipsden, in a loud voice.

"Don't bellow in people's ears. The *Tisbe,* stupid," cried she, screaming at the top of her voice.

"Ri tum, ti turn, ti tum, tum, tum, tiddy, iddy," went Lord Ipsden—he whistled a polka.

Lady Barbara (inspecting him gravely). "I have heard it at a distance, but I never saw how it was done before. *It is very, very pretty!!!!*"

Ipsden. "Polkez-vous, madame?"

Lady Barb. "Si, je polke, Monsieur le Vicomte."

They polked for a second or two.

"Well, I dare say I am wrong," cried Lady Barbara, "but I like you better now you are a downright—ahem!—than when you were only an insipid non-intellectual—you are greatly improved."

Ips. "In what respects?'

Lady Barb. "Did I not tell you? browner and more impudent;

but tell me," said she, resuming her sly, satirical tone, "how is it that you, who used to be the pink of courtesy, dance and sing over the wreck of my fortunes?"

"Because they are not wrecked."

"I thought I told you my specie is gone down in the *Tisbe.*"

Ipsden. "But the *Tisbe* has not gone down."

Lady Barb. "I tell you it is."

Ipsden. "I assure you it is not."

Lady Barb. "It is not?"

Ipsden. "Barbara! I am too happy, I begin to nourish such sweet hopes once more. Oh, I could fall on my knees and bless you for something you said just now."

Lady Barbara blushed to the temples.

"Then why don't you?" said she. "All you want is a little enthusiasm." Then recovering herself, she said:

"You kneel on wet sand, with black trousers on; that will never be!!!"

These two were so occupied that they did not observe the approach of a stranger until he broke in upon their dialogue.

An Ancient Mariner had been for some minutes standing off and on, reconnoitering Lord Ipsden; he now bore down, and with great rough, roaring cordiality, that made Lady Barbara start, cried out:

"Give me your hand, sir—give me your hand, if you were twice a lord.

"I couldn't speak to you till the brig was safe in port, and you slipped away, but I've brought you up at last; and—give me your hand again, sir. I say, isn't it a pity you are a lord instead of a sailor?"

Ipsden. "But I am a sailor."

Ancient Mariner. "That ye are, and as smart a one as ever tied a true-lover's knot in the top; but tell the truth—you were never nearer losing the number of your mess than that day in the old *Tisbe.*"

Lady Barb. "The old *Tisbe!* Oh!"

Ipsden. "Do you remember that nice little lurch she gave to leeward as we brought her round?"

Lady Barb. "Oh, Richard!"

Ancient Mariner. "And that reel the old wench gave under our feet, north the pier-head. I wouldn't have given a washing-tub for her at that moment."

Ipsden. "Past danger becomes pleasure, sir. *Olim et hoc meminisse*—I beg your pardon, sir."

Ancient Mariner (taking off his hat with feeling). "God bless ye, sir, and send ye many happy days, and well spent, with the pretty lady I see alongside; asking your pardon, miss, for parting pleasanter company—so I'll sheer off."

And away went the skipper of the *Tisbe,* rolling fearfully. In the heat of this reminiscence, the skipper of the yacht (they are all alike, blue water once fairly tasted) had lost sight of Lady Barbara; he now looked round. Imagine his surprise!

Her ladyship was in tears.

"Dear Barbara," said Lord Ipsden, "do not distress yourself on my account."

"It is not your fe-feelings I care about; at least, I h-h-hope not; but I have been so unjust, and I prided myself so on my j-ju-justice."

"Never mind!"

"Oh! if you don't, I don't. I hate myself, so it is no wonder you h-hate me."

"I love you more than ever."

"Then you are a good soul! Of course you know I always *l*-esteemed you, Richard."

"No! I had an idea you despised me!"

"How silly you are! Can't you see? When I thought you were not perfection, which you are now, it vexed me to death; you never saw me affront any one but you?"

"No, I never did! What does that prove?"

"That depends upon the wit of him that reasons thereon." (Coming to herself.)

"I love you, Barbara! Will you honor me with your hand?"

"No! I am not so base, so selfish. You are worth a hundred of me, and here have I been treating you *de haut en bas.* Dear Richard, poor Richard. Oh! oh! oh!" (A perfect flood of tears.)

"Barbara! I regret nothing; this moment pays for all."

"Well, then, I will! since you keep pressing me. There, let me go; I must be alone; I must tell the sea how unjust I was, and how happy I am, and when you see me again you shall see the better side of your cousin Barbara."

She was peremptory. "She had her folly and his merits to think over," she said; but she promised to pass through Newhaven, and he should put her into her pony-phaeton, which would meet her there.

Lady Barbara was only a fool by the excess of her wit over her experience; and Lord Ipsden's love was not misplaced, for she had a great heart which she hid from little people. I forgive her!

The resolutions she formed in company with the sea, having dismissed Ipsden, and ordered her flunky into the horizon, will probably give our viscount just half a century of conjugal bliss.

As he was going she stopped him and said: "Your friend had browner hands than I have hitherto conceived possible. *To tell the truth,* I took them for the claws of a mahogany table when he grappled you—is that the term? *C'est e'gal*—I like him—"

She stopped him again. "Ipsden, in the midst of all this that poor man's ship is broken. I feel it is! You will buy him another, if you really love me—for I like him."

And so these lovers parted for a time; and Lord Ipsden with a bounding heart returned to Newhaven. He went to entertain his late *vis-'a-vis* at the "Peacock."

Meantime a shorter and less pleasant *rencontre* had taken place between Leith and that village.

Gatty felt he should meet his lost sweetheart; and sure enough, at a turn of the road Christie and Jean came suddenly upon him.

Jean nodded, but Christie took no notice of him; they passed him; he turned and followed them, and said, "Christie!"

"What is your will wi' me?" said she, coldly.

"I—I— How pale you are!"

"I am no very weel."

"She has been watching over muckle wi' Flucker," said Jean.

Christie thanked her with a look.

"I hope it is not—not—"

"Nae fears, lad," said she, briskly; "I dinna think that muckle o' ye."

"And I think of nothing but you," said he.

A deep flush crimsoned the young woman's brow, but she restrained herself, and said icily: "Thaat's very gude o' ye, I'm sure."

Gatty felt all the contempt her manners and words expressed.

He bit his lips. The tear started to his eye. "You will forget me," said he. "I do not deserve to be remembered, but I shall never forget you. I leave for England. I leave Newhaven forever, where I have been so happy. I am going at three o'clock by the steamboat. Won't you bid me good-by?" He approached her timidly.

"Ay! that wull do," cried she; "Gude be wi' ye, lad; I wish ye nae ill." She gave a commanding gesture of dismissal; he turned away, and went sadly from her. She watched every motion when his back was turned.

"That is you, Christie," said Jean; "use the lads like dirt, an' they think a' the mair o' ye."

"Oh, Jean, my hairt's broken. I'm just deeing for him."

"Let me speak till him then," said Jean; "I'll sune bring him till his marrow-banes;" and she took a hasty step to follow him.

Christie held her fast. "I'd dee ere I'd give in till them. Oh, Jean! I'm a lassie clean flung awa; he has neither hairt nor spunk ava, yon lad!"

Jean began to make excuses for him. Christie inveighed against him. Jean spoke up for him with more earnestness.

Now observe, Jean despised the poor boy.

Christie adored him.

So Jean spoke for him, because women of every degree are often one solid mass of tact; and Christie abused him, because she wanted to hear him defended.

CHAPTER XVI

RICHARD, LORD VISCOUNT IPSDEN, having dotted the seashore with sentinels, to tell him of Lady Barbara's approach, awaited his guest in the "Peacock"; but, as Gatty was a little behind time, he placed Saunders sentinel over the "Peacock," and strolled eastward; as he came out of the "Peacock," Mrs. Gatty came down the little hill in front, and also proceeded eastward; meantime Lady Barbara and her escort were not far from the New Town of Newhaven, on their way from Leith.

Mrs. Gatty came down, merely with a vague fear. She had no reason to suppose her son's alliance with Christie either would or could be renewed, but she was a careful player and would not give a chance away; she found he was gone out unusually early, so she came straight to the only place she dreaded; it was her son's last day in Scotland. She had packed his clothes, and he had inspired her with confidence by arranging pictures, etc., himself; she had no idea he was packing for his departure from this life, not Edinburgh only.

She came then to Newhaven with no serious misgivings, for, even if her son had again vacillated, she saw that, with Christie's pride and her own firmness, the game must be hers in the end; but, as I said before, she was one who played her cards closely, and such seldom lose.

But my story is with the two young fishwives, who, on their return from Leith, found themselves at the foot of the New Town, Newhaven, some minutes before any of the other persons who, it is to be observed, were approaching it from different points; they came slowly in, Christie in particular, with a listlessness she had never, known till this last week; for some days her strength had failed her—it was Jean that carried the creel now—before, Christie, in the pride of her strength, would always do more than her share of their joint labor. Then she could hardly be forced to eat, and what she did eat was quite tasteless to her, and sleep left her, and in its stead came uneasy slumbers, from which she awoke quivering from head to foot.

Oh! perilous venture of those who love one object with the whole heart.

This great but tender heart was breaking day by day.

Well, Christie and Jean, strolling slowly into the New Town of Newhaven, found an assemblage of the natives all looking seaward; the fishermen, except Sandy Liston, were away at the herring fishery, but all the boys and women of the New Town were collected; the girls felt a momentary curiosity; it proved, however, to be only an individual swimming in toward shore from a greater distance than usual.

A little matter excites curiosity in such places.

The man's head looked like a spot of ink.

Sandy Liston was minding his own business, lazily mending a skait-net, which he had attached to a crazy old herring-boat hauled up to rot.

Christie sat down, pale and languid, by him, on a creepie that

Charles Reade

a lass who had been baiting a line with mussels had just vacated; suddenly she seized Jean's arm with a convulsive motion; Jean looked up—it was the London steamboat running out from Leith to Granton Pier to take up her passengers for London. Charles Gatty was going by that boat; the look of mute despair the poor girl gave went to Jean's heart; she ran hastily from the group, and cried out of sight for poor Christie.

A fishwife, looking through a telescope at the swimmer, remarked: "He's coming in fast; he's a gallant swimmer, yon—

"Can he dee't?" inquired Christie of Sandy Liston.

"Fine thaat," was the reply; "he does it aye o' Sundays when ye are at the kirk."

"It's no oot o' the kirk window ye'll hae seen him, Sandy, my mon," said a young fishwife.

"Rin for my glass ony way, Flucker," said Christie, forcing herself to take some little interest.

Flucker brought it to her, she put her hand on his shoulder, got slowly up, and stood on the creepie and adjusted the focus of her glass; after a short view, she said to Flucker:

"Rin and see the nook." She then leveled her glass again at the swimmer.

Flucker informed her the nook said "half eleven"—Scotch for "half past ten."

Christie whipped out a well-thumbed almanac.

"Yon nook's aye ahint," said she. She swept the sea once more with her glass, then brought it together with a click, and jumped off the stool. Her quick intelligence viewed the matter differently from all the others.

"Noow," cried she, smartly, "wha'll lend me his yawl?"

"Hets! dinna be sae interferin', lassie," said a fishwife.

"Hae nane o' ye ony spunk?" said Christie, taking no notice of the woman. "Speak, laddies!"

"M' uncle's yawl is at the pier-head; ye'll get her, my woman," said a boy.

"A schell'n for wha's first on board," said Christie, holding up the coin.

"Come awa', Flucker, we'll hae her schell'n;" and these two worthies instantly effected a false start.

"It's no under your jackets," said Christie, as she dashed after them like the wind.

"Haw! haw! haw!" laughed Sandy.

"What's her business picking up a mon against his will?" said a woman.

"She's an awfu' lassie," whined another. The examination of the swimmer was then continued, and the crowd increased; some would have it he was rapidly approaching, others that he made little or no way.

"Wha est?" said another.

"It's a lummy," said a girl.

"Na! it's no a lummy," said another.

Christie's boat was now seen standing out from the pier. Sandy Liston, casting a contemptuous look on all the rest, lifted himself lazily into the herring-boat and looked seaward. His manner changed in a moment.

"The Deevil!" cried he; "the tide's turned! You wi' your glass, could you no see yon man's drifting oot to sea?"

"Hech!" cried the women, "he'll be drooned—he'll be drooned!"

"Yes; he'll be drooned!" cried Sandy, "if yon lassie does na come alongside him deevelich quick—he's sair spent, I doot."

Two spectators were now added to the scene, Mrs. Gatty and Lord Ipsden. Mrs. Gatty inquired what was the matter.

"It's a mon drooning," was the reply.

The poor fellow, whom Sandy, by aid of his glass, now discovered to be in a wornout condition, was about half a mile east of Newhaven pier-head, and unfortunately the wind was nearly due east. Christie was standing north-northeast, her boat-hook jammed against the sail, which stood as flat as a knife.

The natives of the Old Town were now seen pouring down to the pier and the beach, and strangers were collecting like bees.

"After wit is everybody's wit!!!"—*Old Proverb.*

The affair was in the Johnstone's hands.

"That boat is not going to the poor man," said Mrs. Gatty, "it is turning its back upon him."

"She canna lie in the wind's eye, for as clever as she is," answered a fishwife.

"I ken wha it is," suddenly squeaked a little fishwife; "it's Christie Johnstone's lad; it's yon daft painter fr' England. Hech!" cried she, suddenly, observing Mrs. Gatty, "it's your son, woman."

The unfortunate woman gave a fearful scream, and, flying like a tiger on Liston, commanded him "to go straight out to sea and save her son."

Jean Carnie seized her arm. "Div ye see yon boat?" cried she; "and div ye mind Christie, the lass wha's hairt ye hae broken? aweel, woman—*it's just a race between deeth and Cirsty Johnstone for your son.*

The poor old woman swooned dead away; they carried her into Christie Johnstone's house and laid her down, then hurried back—the greater terror absorbed the less.

Lady Barbara Sinclair was there from Leith; and, seeing Lord Ipsden standing in the boat with a fisherman, she asked him to tell her what it was; neither he nor any one answered her.

"Why doesn't she come about, Liston ?" cried Lord Ipsden, stamping with anxiety and impatience.

"She'll no be lang," said Sandy; "but they'll mak a mess o' 't wi' ne'er a man i' the boat."

"Ye're sure o' thaat?" put in a woman.

"Ay, about she comes," said Liston, as the sail came down on the first tack. He was mistaken; they dipped the lug as cleverly as any man in the town could.

"Hech! look at her hauling on the rope like a mon," cried a woman. The sail flew up on the other tack.

"She's an awfu' lassie,". whined another.

"He's awa," groaned Liston, "he's doon!"

"No! he's up again," cried Lord Ipsden; "but I fear he can't live till the boat comes to him."

The fisherman and the viscount held on by each other.

"He does na see her, or maybe he'd tak hairt."

"I'd give ten thousand pounds if only he could see her. My God, the man will be drowned under our eyes. If he but saw her!!!"

The words had hardly left Lord Ipsden's lips, when the sound of a woman's voice came like an AEolian note across the water.

"Hurraih!" roared Liston, and every creature joined the cheer.

"She'll no let him dee. Ah! she's in the bows, hailing him an' waving the lad's bonnet ower her head to gie him coorage. Gude bless ye, lass; Gude bless ye!"

Christie knew it was no use hailing him against the wind, but the moment she got the wind she darted into the bows, and pitched in its highest key her full and brilliant voice; after a moment of suspense she received proof that she must be heard by him, for on the pier now hung men and women, clustered like bees, breathless with anxiety, and the moment after she hailed the drowning man, she saw and heard a wild yell of applause burst from the pier, and the pier was more distant than the man. She snatched Flucker's cap, planted her foot on the gunwale, held on by a rope, hailed the poor fellow again, and waved the cap round and round her head, to give him courage; and in a moment, at the sight of this, thousands of voices thundered back their cheers to her across the water. Blow, wind—spring, boat—and you, Christie, still ring life toward those despairing ears and wave hope to those sinking eyes; cheer the boat on, you thousands that look upon this action; hurrah! from the pier; hurrah! from the town; hurrah! from the shore; hurrah! now, from the very ships in the roads, whose crews are swarming on the yards to look; five minutes ago they laughed at you; three thousand eyes and hearts hang upon you now; ay, these are the moments we live for!

And now dead silence. The boat is within fifty yards, they are all three consulting together round the mast; an error now is death; his forehead only seems above water.

"If they miss him on that tack?" said Lord Ipsden, significantly, to Liston.

"He'll never see London Brigg again," was the whispered reply.

They carried on till all on shore thought they would run over him, or past him; but no, at ten yards distant they were all at the sail, and had it down like lightning; and then Flucker sprang to the bows, the other boy to the helm.

Unfortunately, there were but two Johnstones in the boat; and this boy, in his hurry, actually put the helm to port, instead of to starboard. Christie, who stood amidships, saw the error; she sprang aft, flung the boy from the helm and jammed it hard-a-starboard with her foot. The boat answered the helm, but too late for Flucker; the man was four yards from him as the boat drifted by.

"He's a deed mon!" cried Liston, on shore.

The boat's length gave one more little chance; the after-part must drift nearer him—thanks to Christie. Flucker flew aft; flung himself on his back, and seized his sister's petticoats.

"Fling yourself ower the gunwale," screamed he. "Ye'll no hurt; I'se haud ye."

She flung herself boldly over the gunwale; the man was sinking, her nails touched his hair, her fingers entangled themselves in it, she gave him a powerful wrench and brought him alongside; the boys pinned him like wild-cats.

Christie darted away forward to the mast, passed a rope round it, threw it the boys, in a moment it was under his shoulders. Christie hauled on it from the fore thwart, the boys lifted him, and they tumbled him, gasping and gurgling like a dying salmon, into the bottom of the boat, and flung net and jackets and sail over him to keep the life in him.

Ah! draw your breath all hands at sea and ashore, and don't try it again, young gentleman, for there was nothing to spare; when you were missed at the bow two stout hearts quivered for you; Lord Ipsden hid his face in his two hands, Sandy Liston gave a groan, and, when you were grabbed astern, jumped out of his boat and cried:

"A gill o' whisky for ony favor, for it's turned me as seeck as a doeg." He added: "He may bless yon lassie's fowr banes, for she's ta'en him oot o' Death's maw, as sure as Gude's in heaven!"

Lady Barbara, who had all her life been longing to see perilous adventures, prayed and trembled and cried most piteously; and Lord Ipsden's back was to her, and he paid no attention to her voice; but when the battle was won, and Lord Ipsden turned and saw her, she clung to his arm and dried her tears; and then the Old Town cheered the boat, and the New Town cheered the boat, and the towns cheered each other; and the Johnstones, lad and lass, set their sail, and swept back in triumph to the pier; so then Lady Barbara's blood mounted and tingled in her veins like fire. "Oh, how noble!" cried she.

"Yes, dearest," said Ipsden. "You have seen something great done at last; and by a woman, too!"

"Yes," said Barbara, "how beautiful! oh! how beautiful it all is; only the next one I see I should like the danger to be over first, that is all."

The boys and Christie, the moment they had saved Gatty, up sail again for Newhaven; they landed in about three minutes at the pier.

TIME. From Newhaven town to pier on foot: 1 m. 30 sec. First tack: 5 m. 30 sec. Second tack, and getting him on board: 4 m. 0 sec. Back to the pier, going free: 3 m. 30 sec.

Total: 14 m. 30 sec.

They came in to the pier, Christie sitting quietly on the thwart after her work, the boy steering, and Flucker standing against the mast, hands in his pockets; the deportment this young gentleman thought fit to assume on this occasion was "complete apathy"; he came into port with the air of one bringing home the ordinary results of his day's fishing; this was, I suppose, to impress the spectators with the notion that saving lives was an every-day affair with La Famille Johnstone; as for Gatty, he came to himself under his heap of nets and jackets and spoke once between Death's jaw and the pier.

"Beautiful!" murmured he, and was silent. The meaning of this observation never transpired, and never will in this world. Six months afterward, being subjected to a searching interrogatory, he stated that he had alluded to the majesty and freedom of a certain *pose* Christie had adopted while hailing him from the boat; but, reader, if he had wanted you and me to believe it was this, he should not have been half a year finding it out—*increduli odimus!* They landed, and Christie sprang on shore; while she was wending her way through the crowd, impeded by greetings and acclamations, with every now and then a lass waving her kerchief or a lad his bonnet over the heroine's head, poor Mrs. Gatty was receiving the attention of the New Town; they brought her to, they told her the good news—she thanked God.

The whole story had spread like wildfire; they expostulated with her, they told her now was the time to show she had a heart, and bless the young people.

She rewarded them with a valuable precept.

"Mind your own business!" said she.

"Hech! y' are a dour wife!" cried Newhaven.

The dour wife bent her eyes on the ground.

The people were still collected at the foot of the street, but they were now in knots, when in dashed Flucker, arriving by a short cut, and crying: "She does na ken, she does na ken, she was ower moedest to look, I daur say, and ye'll no tell her, for he's a blackguard, an' he's just making a fule o' the puir lass, and if she kens what she has done for him, she'll be fonder o' him than a coow o' her cauf."

"Oh, Flucker! we maun tell her, it's her lad, her ain lad, she saved," expostulated a woman.

"Did ever my feyther do a good turn till ye?" cried Flucker. "Awel, then, ye'll no tell the lassie, she's weel as she is; he's gaun t' Enngland the day. I cannie gie ye a' a hidin'," said he, with an eye that flashed volumes of good intention on a hundred and fifty people; "but I am feytherless and motherless, an' I can fa' on my knees an' curse ye a' if ye do us sic an ill turn, an' then ye'll see whether ye'll thrive."

"We'll no tell, Flucker, ye need na curse us ony way."

His lordship, with all the sharp authority of a skipper, ordered Master Flucker to the pier, with a message to the yacht; Flucker *qua* yachtsman was a machine, and went as a matter of course. "I am determined to tell her," said Lord Ipsden to Lady Barbara.

"But," remonstrated Lady Barbara, "the poor boy says he will curse us if we do."

"He won't curse me."

"How do you know that?"

"Because the little blackguard's grog would be stopped on board the yacht if he did."

Charles Reade

Flucker had not been gone many minutes before loud cheering was heard, and Christie Johnstone appeared convoyed by a large detachment of the Old Town; she had tried to slip away, but they would not let her. They convoyed her in triumph till they saw the New Town people, and then they turned and left her.

She came in among the groups, a changed woman—her pallor and her listlessness were gone—the old light was in her eye, and the bright color in her cheek, and she seemed hardly to touch the earth.

"I'm just droukit, lasses," cried she, gayly, wringing her sleeve. Every eye was upon her; did she know, or did she not know, what she had done?

Lord Ipsden stepped forward; the people tacitly accepted him as the vehicle of their curiosity.

"Who was it, Christie?"

"I dinna ken, for my pairt!"

Mrs. Gatty came out of the house.

"A handsome young fellow, I hope, Christie?" resumed Lord Ipsden.

"Ye maun ask Flucker," was the reply. "I could no tak muckle notice, ye ken," putting her hand before her eye, and half smiling.

"Well! I hear he is very good-looking; and I hear you think so, too."

She glided to him and looked in his face. He gave a meaning

smile. The poor girl looked quite perplexed. Suddenly she gave a violent start.

"Christie! where is Christie?" had cried a well-known voice. He had learned on the pier who had saved him—he had slipped up among the boats to find her—he could not find his hat—he could not wait for it—his dripping hair showed where he had been—it was her love whom she had just saved out of Death's very jaws.

She gave a cry of love that went through every heart, high or low, young or old, that heard it. And she went to him, through the air it seemed; but, quick as she was, another was as quick; the mother had seen him first, and she was there. Christie saw nothing. With another cry, the very keynote of her great and loving heart, she flung her arms round—Mrs. Gatty, who was on the same errand as herself.

"Hearts are not steel, and steel is bent; Hearts are not flint, and flint is rent."

The old woman felt Christie touch her. She turned from her son in a moment and wept upon her neck. Her lover took her hand and kissed it, and pressed it to his bosom, and tried to speak to her; but all he could do was to sob and choke—and kiss her hand again.

"My daughter!" sobbed the old woman.

At that word Christie clasped her quickly; and then Christie began to cry.

"I am not a stone," cried Mrs. Gatty.

"I gave him life; but you have saved him from death. Oh, Charles, never make her repent what she has done for you."

She was a woman, after all; and prudence and prejudice melted like snow before her heart.

There were not many dry eyes—least of all the heroic Lady Barbara's.

The three whom a moment had made one were becoming calmer, and taking one another's hands for life, when a diabolical sound arose—and what was it but Sandy Liston, who, after furious resistance, was blubbering with explosive but short-lived violence? Having done it, he was the first to draw everybody's attention to the phenomenon; and affecting to consider it a purely physical attack, like a *coup de soleil,* or so on, he proceeded instantly to Drysel's for his panacea.

Lady Barbara enjoined Lord Ipsden to watch these people, and not to lose a word they said; and, after she had insisted upon kissing Christie, she went off to her carriage. And she too was so happy, she cried three distinct times on her way to Edinburgh.

Lord Ipsden, having reminded Gatty of his engagement, begged him to add his mother and Christie to the party, and escorted Lady Barbara to her phaeton.

So then the people dispersed by degrees.

"That old lady's face seems familiar to me," said Lord Ipsden, as he stood on the little natural platform by the "Peacock." "Do you know who she is, Saunders?"

"It is Peggy, that was cook in your lordship's uncle's time, my lord. She married a green-grocer," added Saunders, with an injured air.

"Hech! hech!" cried Flucker, "Christie has ta'en up her head wi' a cook's son."

Mrs. Gatty was ushered into the "Peacock" with mock civility by Mr. Saunders. No recognition took place, each being ashamed of the other as an acquaintance.

The next arrival was a beautiful young lady in a black silk gown, a plain but duck-like plaid shawl, who proved to be Christie Johnstone, in her Sunday attire.

When they met, Mrs. Gatty gave a little scream of joy, and said: "Oh, my child; if I had seen you in that dress, I should never have said a word against you."

"Pars minima est ipsa puella sui!"

His lordship stepped up to her, took off his hat, and said: "Will Mrs. Gatty take from me a commission for two pictures, as big as herself, and as bonny?" added he, doing a little Scotch. He handed her a check; and, turning to Gatty, added, "At your convenience, sir, *bien entendu.*"

"Hech! it's for five hundred pund, Chairles."

"Good gear gangs in little book,"* said Jean.

*Bulk.

"Ay, does it," replied Flucker, assuming the compliment.

"My lord!" said the artist, "you treat Art like a prince; and she shall treat you like a queen. When the sun comes out again, I will work for you and fame. You shall have two things painted, every stroke loyally in the sunlight. In spite of gloomy winter and gloomier London, I will try if I can't hang nature and summer on your walls forever. As for me, you know I must go to Gerard Dow and Cuyp, and Pierre de Hoogh, when my little sand is run; but my handwriting shall warm your children's children's hearts, sir, when this hand is dust." His eye turned inward, he walked to and fro, and his companions died out of his sight—he was in the kingdom of art.

His lordship and Jean entered the "Peacock," followed by Flucker, who merely lingered at the door to moralize as follows:

"Hech! hech! isna thaat lamentable? Christie's mon's as daft as a drunk weaver."

But one stayed quietly behind, and assumed that moment the office of her life.

"Ay!" he burst out again, "the resources of our art are still unfathomed! Pictures are yet to be painted that shall refresh men's inner souls, and help their hearts against the artificial world; and charm the fiend away, like David's harp!! The world, after centuries of lies, will give nature and truth a trial. What a paradise art will be, when truths, instead of lies, shall be told on paper, on marble, on canvas, and on the boards!!!"

"Dinner's on the boarrd," murmured Christie, alluding to Lord Ipsden's breakfast; "and I hae the charge o' ye," pulling his sleeve hard enough to destroy the equilibrium of a flea.

"Then don't let us waste our time here. Oh, Christie!"

"What est, my laddy?"

"I'm so preciously hungry!!!!"

"C-way* then!"

* Come away.

Off they ran, hand in hand, sparks of beauty, love and happiness flying all about them.

CHAPTER XVII

"THERE is nothing but meeting and parting in this world!" and you may be sure the incongruous personages of our tale could not long be together. Their separate paths had met for an instant in one focus, furnished then and there the matter of an eccentric story, and then diverged forever.

Our lives have a general current, and also an episode or two; and the episodes of a commonplace life are often rather startling; in like manner this tale is not a specimen, but an episode of Lord Ipsden and Lady Barbara, who soon after this married and lived like the rest of the *beau monde*. In so doing, they passed out of my hands; such as wish to know how viscounts and viscountesses feed and sleep, and do the domestic (so called), and the social (so called), are referred to the fashionable novel. To Mr. Saunders, for instance, who has in the press one of those cerberus-leviathans of fiction, so common now; incredible as folio to future ages. Saunders will take you by the hand, and lead you over carpets two inches thick—under rosy curtains—to dinner-tables. He will *fete* you, and opera you, and dazzle your young imagination with *e'p'ergnes,* and salvers, and buhl and ormolu. No fishwives or painters shall intrude upon his polished scenes; all shall be as genteel as himself. Saunders is a good authority; he is more in the society, and far more in the confidence of the great, than most fashionable novelists. Mr.

Saunders's work will be in three volumes; nine hundred and ninety pages!!!!!!

In other words, this single work of this ingenious writer will equal in bulk the aggregate of all the writings extant by Moses, David, Solomon, Isaiah, and St. Paul!!!

I shall not venture into competition with this behemoth of the *salon;* I will evaporate in thin generalities.

Lord Ipsden then lived very happily with Lady Barbara, whose hero he straightway became, and who nobly and poetically dotes upon him. He has gone into political life to please her, and will remain there—to please himself. They were both very grateful to Newhaven; when they married they vowed to visit it twice a year, and mingle a fortnight's simple life with its simple scenes; but four years have passed, and they have never been there again, and I dare say never will; but when Viscount Ipsden falls in with a brother aristocrat who is crushed by the fiend *ennui,* he remembers Aberford, and condenses his famous recipe into a two-edged hexameter, which will make my learned reader laugh, for it is full of wisdom:

"Diluculo surgas! miseris succurrere discas!!"

Flucker Johnstone meditated during breakfast upon the five hundred pounds, and regretted he had not years ago adopted Mr. Gatty's profession; some days afterward he invited his sister to a conference. Chairs being set, Mr. Flucker laid down this observation, that near relations should be deuced careful not to cast discredit upon one another; that now his sister was to be a lady, it was repugnant to his sense of right to be a fisherman and make her ladyship blush for him; on the contrary, he felt it his duty to rise to such high consideration that she should be proud of him.

Christie acquiesced at once in this position, but professed herself embarrassed to know how such a "ne'er-do-weel" was to be made a source of pride; then she kissed Flucker, and said, in a tone somewhat inconsistent with the above, "Tell me, my laamb!"

Her lamb informed her that the sea has many paths; some of them disgraceful, such as line or net fishing, and the periodical laying down, on rocky shoals, and taking up again, of lobster-creels; others, superior to anything the dry land can offer in importance and dignity and general estimation, such as the command of a merchant vessel trading to the East or West Indies. Her lamb then suggested that if she would be so good as to launch him in the merchant-service, with a good rig of clothes and money in his pocket, there was that in his head which would enable him to work to windward of most of his contemporaries. He bade her calculate upon the following results: In a year or two he would be second mate, and next year first mate, and in a few years more skipper! Think of that, lass! Skipper of a vessel, whose rig he generously left his sister free to determine; premising that two masts were, in his theory of navigation, indispensable, and that three were a great deal more like Cocker than two. This led to a general consultation; Flucker's ambition was discussed and praised. That modest young gentleman, in spite of many injunctions to the contrary, communicated his sister's plans for him to Lord Ipsden, and affected to doubt their prudence. The bait took; Lord Ipsden wrote to his man of business, and an unexpected blow fell upon the ingenious Flucker. He was sent to school; there to learn a little astronomy, a little navigation, a little seamanship, a little manners, etc.; in the mysteries of reading and writing his sister had already perfected him by dint of "the taws." This school was a blow; but Flucker was no fool; he saw there was no way of getting from school to sea without working. So he literally worked out to sea. His first voyage was distinguished by the following peculiarities: Attempts to put tricks upon this particular novice generally ended in the laugh turning against the experimenters; and instead of drinking his grog, which he hates, he secreted it, and sold it for various advantages. He has been now four voyages. When he comes ashore, instead of going to haunts of folly and vice, he instantly bears up for his sister's house—Kensington Gravel-pits—which he makes in the following manner: He goes up the river—Heaven knows where all—this he calls running down the longitude; then he lands, and bears down upon the Gravel-pits; in particular knowledge of the names of streets he is deficient, but he knows the exact bearings of Christie's dwelling. He tacks and wears according as masonry compels him, and he arrives at the gate. He hails the house, in a voice that brings all the inhabitants of the row to their windows, including Christie; he is fallen upon and dragged into the house. The first thing is, he draws out from his boots, and his back, and other hiding-places, China crape and marvelous silk handkerchiefs for Christie; and she takes from his pocket a mass of Oriental sugar-plums, with which, but for this precaution, she knows by experience he would poison young Charley; and soon he is to be seen sitting with his hand in his sister's, and she lookng like a mother upon his handsome, weather-beaten face, and Gatty opposite, adoring him as a specimen of male beauty, and sometimes making furtive sketches of him. And then the tales he always brings with him; the house is never very dull, but it is livelier than ever when this inexhaustible sailor casts anchor in it.

The friends (chiefly artists) who used to leave at 9:30, stay till eleven; for an intelligent sailor is better company than two lawyers, two bishops, three soldiers, and four writers of plays and tales, all rolled together. And still he tells Christie he shall command a vessel some day, and leads her to the most cheering inferences from the fact of his prudence and his general width-awake; in particular he bids her contrast with him the general fate of sailors, eaten up by land-sharks, particularly of the female gender, whom he demonstrates to be the worst enemies poor Jack has; he calls these sunken rocks, fire-ships and other metaphors. He concludes thus: "You are all the lass I mean to have till I'm a skipper, and then I'll bear up alongside some pretty, decent lass, like yourself, Christie, and we'll sail in company all our lives, let the wind blow high or low." Such is the gracious Flucker become in his twentieth year. Last voyage, with Christie's aid, he produced a sextant of his own, and "made it twelve o'clock" (with the sun's consent, I hope), and the eyes of authority fell upon him. So, who knows? perhaps he may one day, sail a ship; and, if he does, he will be prouder and happier than if we made him monarch of the globe.

To return to our chiefs; Mrs. Gatty gave her formal consent to her son's marriage with Christie Johnstone.

There were examples. Aristocracy had ere now condescended to wealth; earls had married women rich by tallow-importing papas; and no doubt, had these same earls been consulted in Gatty's case, they would have decided that Christie Johnstone, with her real and funded property, was not a villainous match for a green grocer's son, without a rapp;* but Mrs. Gatty did not reason so, did not reason at all, luckily, her heart ran away with her judgment, and, her judgment ceasing to act, she became a wise woman.

*A diminutive German coin.

The case was peculiar. Gatty was a artist *pur sang*—and Christie, who would not have been the wife for a *petit maitre,* was the wife of wives for him.

He wanted a beautiful wife to embellish his canvas,

disfigured hitherto by an injudicious selection of models; a virtuous wife to be his crown; a prudent wife to save him from ruin; a cheerful wife to sustain his spirits, drooping at times by virtue of his artist's temperament; an intellectual wife to preserve his children from being born dolts and bred dunces, and to keep his own mind from sharpening to one point, and so contracting and becoming monomaniacal. And he found all these qualities, together with the sun and moon of human existence—true love and true religion—in Christie Johnstone.

In similar cases, foolish men have set to work to make, in six months, their diamond of nature, the exact cut and gloss of other men's pastes, and, nervously watching the process, have suffered torture; luckily Charles Gatty was not wise enough for this; he saw nature had distinguished her he loved beyond her fellows; here, as elsewhere, he had faith in nature—he believed that Christie would charm everybody of eye, and ear, and mind, and heart, that approached her; he admired her as she was, and left her to polish herself, if she chose. He did well; she came to London with a fine mind, a broad brogue, a delicate ear; she observed how her husband's friends spoke, and in a very few months she had toned down her Scotch to a rich Ionic coloring, which her womanly instinct will never let her exchange for the thin, vinegar accents that are too prevalent in English and French society; and in other respects she caught, by easy gradation, the tone of the new society to which her marriage introduced her, without, however, losing her charming self.

The wise dowager lodges hard by, having resisted an invitation to be in the same house; she comes to that house to assist the young wife with her experience, and to be welcome—not to interfere every minute, and tease her; she loves her daughter-in-law almost as much as she does her son, and she is happy because he bids fair to be an immortal painter, and, above all, a gentleman; and she, a wifely wife, a motherly mother, and, above all, a lady.

This, then, is a happy couple. Their life is full of purpose and industry, yet lightened by gayety; they go to operas, theaters and balls, for they are young. They have plenty of society, real society, not the ill-assorted collection of a predetermined number of bodies, that blindly assumes that name, but the rich communication of various and fertile minds; they very, very seldom consent to squat four mortal hours on one chair (like old hares stiffening in their hot forms), and nibbling, sipping and twaddling in four mortal hours what could have been eaten, drunken and said in thirty-five minutes. They are both artists at heart, and it shocks their natures to see folks mix so very largely the *inutile* with the *insipidum,* and waste, at one huge but barren incubation, the soul, and the stomach, and the irrevocable hours, things with which so much is to be done. But they have many desirable acquaintances, and not a few friends; the latter are mostly lovers of truth in their several departments, and in all things. Among them are painters, sculptors, engineers, writers, conversers, thinkers; these acknowledging, even in England, other gods besides the intestines, meet often *chez* Gatty, chiefly for mental intercourse; a cup of tea with such is found, by experience, to be better than a stalled elk where chit-chat reigns over the prostrate hours.

This, then, is a happy couple; the very pigeons and the crows need not blush for the nest at Kensington Gravel-pits. There the divine institution Marriage takes its natural colors, and it is at once pleasant and good to catch such glimpses of Heaven's design, and sad to think how often this great boon, accorded by God to man and woman, must have been abused and perverted, ere it could have sunk to be the standing butt of farce-writers, and the theme of weekly punsters.

In this pair we see the wonders a male and female can do for each other in the sweet bond of holy wedlock. In that blessed relation alone two interests are really one, and two hearts lie safe at anchor side by side.

Christie and Charles are friends—for they are man and wife.

Christie and Charles are lovers still—for they are man and wife.

Christie and Charles are one forever—for they are man and wife.

This wife brightens the house, from kitchen to garret, for her husband; this husband works like a king for his wife's comfort, and for his own fame—and that fame is his wife's glory. When one of these expresses or hints a wish, the other's first impulse is to find the means, not the objections.

They share all troubles, and, by sharing, halve them.

They share all pleasures, and, by sharing, double them.

They climb the hill together now, and many a canty day they shall have with one another; and when, by the inevitable law, they begin to descend toward the dark valley, they will still go hand in hand, smiling so tenderly, and supporting each other with a care more lovely than when the arm was strong and the foot firm.

On these two temperate lives old age will descend lightly, gradually, gently, and late—and late upon these evergreen hearts, because they are not tuned to some selfish, isolated key; these hearts beat and ring with the young hearts of their dear children, and years hence papa and mamma will begin life hopefully, wishfully, warmly again with each loved novice in turn.

And when old age does come, it will be no calamity to these, as it is to you, poor battered beau, laughed at by the fair ninnies who erst laughed with you; to you, poor follower of salmon, fox, and pheasant, whose joints are stiffening, whose nerve is gone—whose Golgotha remains; to you, poor faded beauty, who have staked all upon man's appetite, and not accumulated goodness or sense for your second course; to you, poor drawing-room wit, whose sarcasm has turned to venom and is turning to drivel.

What terrors has old age for this happy pair? it cannot make them ugly, for, though the purple light of youth recedes, a new kind of tranquil beauty, the aloe-blossom of many years of innocence, comes to, and sits like a dove upon, the aged faces, where goodness, sympathy and intelligence have harbored together so long; and where evil passions have flitted (for we are all human), but found no resting-place.

Old age is no calamity to them. It cannot terrify them; for ere they had been married a week the woman taught the man, lover of truth, to search for the highest and greatest truths in a book written for men's souls by the Author of the world, the sea, the stars, the sun, the soul; and this book, *Dei gratia,* will, as the good bishop sings,

"Teach them to live that they may dread The grave as little as their bed."

It cannot make them sad, for, ere it comes loved souls will have gone from earth and from their tender bosom, but not from their memories; and will seem to beckon them now across the cold valley to the golden land.

It cannot make them sad, for on earth the happiest must drink a sorrowful cup more than once in a long life, and so their brightest hopes will have come to dwell habitually on things beyond the grave; and the great painter, *jam Senex,* will chiefly meditate upon a richer landscape and brighter figures than human hand has ever painted; a scene whose glories he can see from hence but by glimpses and through a glass darkly; the great meadows on the other side of Jordan, which are bright with the spirits of the just that walk there, and are warmed with an eternal sun, and ring with the triumph of the humble and the true, and the praises of God forever.

Charles Reade

ABOUT THE AUTHOR

 **Charles Reade** (June 8, 1814 - April 11, 1884) was an English novelist and dramatist, best known for The Cloister and the Hearth.

Reade, the son of an Oxfordshire squire, was born at Ipsden, Oxfordshire. He studied at Magdalen College, Oxford, taking his B.A. in 1835, and became a fellow of his college. He was subsequently dean of arts and vice-president, taking his degree of D.C.L. in 1847. His name was entered at Lincoln's Inn in 1836; he was elected Vinerian Fellow in 1842, and was called to the bar in 1843. He kept his fellowship at Magdalen all his life, but after taking his degree he spent most of his time in London.

He began his literary career as a dramatist, and it was his own wish that the word "dramatist" should stand-first in the description of his occupations on his tombstone. As an author, he always had an eye to stage-effect in scene and situation as well as in dialogue.

He made his name as a novelist in 1856, when he produced It's Never Too Late to Mend, a novel written with the purpose of reforming abuses in prison discipline and the treatment of criminals. Five minor novels followed in quick succession. In 1861 Reade produced what would become his most famous work, The Cloister and the Hearth.

Choose from Thousands of 1stWorldLibrary Classics By

A. M. Barnard
Ada Leverson
Adolphus William Ward
Aesop
Agatha Christie
Alexander Aaronsohn
Alexander Kielland
Alexandre Dumas
Alfred Gatty
Alfred Ollivant
Alice Duer Miller
Alice Turner Curtis
Alice Dunbar
Allen Chapman
Alleyne Ireland
Ambrose Bierce
Amelia E. Barr
Amory H. Bradford
Andrew Lang
Andrew McFarland Davis
Andy Adams
Angela Brazil
Anna Alice Chapin
Anna Sewell
Annie Besant
Annie Hamilton Donnell
Annie Payson Call
Annie Roe Carr
Annonaymous
Anton Chekhov
Archibald Lee Fletcher
Arnold Bennett
Arthur C. Benson
Arthur Conan Doyle
Arthur M. Winfield
Arthur Ransome
Arthur Schnitzler
Arthur Train
Atticus
B.H. Baden-Powell
B. M. Bower
B. C. Chatterjee
Baroness Emmuska Orczy
Baroness Orczy
Basil King
Bayard Taylor
Ben Macomber
Bertha Muzzy Bower
Bjornstjerne Bjornson

Booth Tarkington
Boyd Cable
Bram Stoker
C. Collodi
C. E. Orr
C. M. Ingleby
Carolyn Wells
Catherine Parr Traill
Charles A. Eastman
Charles Amory Beach
Charles Dickens
Charles Dudley Warner
Charles Farrar Browne
Charles Ives
Charles Kingsley
Charles Klein
Charles Hanson Towne
Charles Lathrop Pack
Charles Romyn Dake
Charles Whibley
Charles Willing Beale
Charlotte M. Braeme
Charlotte M. Yonge
Charlotte Perkins Stetson
Clair W. Hayes
Clarence Day Jr.
Clarence E. Mulford
Clemence Housman
Confucius
Coningsby Dawson
Cornelis DeWitt Wilcox
Cyril Burleigh
D. H. Lawrence
Daniel Defoe
David Garnett
Dinah Craik
Don Carlos Janes
Donald Keyhoe
Dorothy Kilner
Dougan Clark
Douglas Fairbanks
E. Nesbit
E. P. Roe
E. Phillips Oppenheim
E. S. Brooks
Earl Barnes
Edgar Rice Burroughs
Edith Van Dyne
Edith Wharton

Edward Everett Hale
Edward J. O'Biren
Edward S. Ellis
Edwin L. Arnold
Eleanor Atkins
Eleanor Hallowell Abbott
Eliot Gregory
Elizabeth Gaskell
Elizabeth McCracken
Elizabeth Von Arnim
Ellem Key
Emerson Hough
Emilie F. Carlen
Emily Bronte
Emily Dickinson
Enid Bagnold
Enilor Macartney Lane
Erasmus W. Jones
Ernie Howard Pie
Ethel May Dell
Ethel Turner
Ethel Watts Mumford
Eugene Sue
Eugenie Foa
Eugene Wood
Eustace Hale Ball
Evelyn Everett-green
Everard Cotes
F. H. Cheley
F. J. Cross
F. Marion Crawford
Fannie E. Newberry
Federick Austin Ogg
Ferdinand Ossendowski
Fergus Hume
Florence A. Kilpatrick
Fremont B. Deering
Francis Bacon
Francis Darwin
Frances Hodgson Burnett
Frances Parkinson Keyes
Frank Gee Patchin
Frank Harris
Frank Jewett Mather
Frank L. Packard
Frank V. Webster
Frederic Stewart Isham
Frederick Trevor Hill
Frederick Winslow Taylor

Friedrich Kerst
Friedrich Nietzsche
Fyodor Dostoyevsky
G.A. Henty
G.K. Chesterton
Gabrielle E. Jackson
Garrett P. Serviss
Gaston Leroux
George A. Warren
George Ade
George Bernard Shaw
George Cary Eggleston
George Durston
George Ebers
George Eliot
George Gissing
George MacDonald
George Meredith
George Orwell
George Sylvester Viereck
George Tucker
George W. Cable
George Wharton James
Gertrude Atherton
Gordon Casserly
Grace E. King
Grace Gallatin
Grace Greenwood
Grant Allen
Guillermo A. Sherwell
Gulielma Zollinger
Gustav Flaubert
H. A. Cody
H. B. Irving
H. C. Bailey
H. G. Wells
H. H. Munro
H. Irving Hancock
H. R. Naylor
H. Rider Haggard
H. W. C. Davis
Haldeman Julius
Hall Caine
Hamilton Wright Mabie
Hans Christian Andersen
Harold Avery
Harold McGrath
Harriet Beecher Stowe
Harry Castlemon
Harry Coghill
Harry Houidini

Hayden Carruth
Helent Hunt Jackson
Helen Nicolay
Hendrik Conscience
Hendy David Thoreau
Henri Barbusse
Henrik Ibsen
Henry Adams
Henry Ford
Henry Frost
Henry James
Henry Jones Ford
Henry Seton Merriman
Henry W Longfellow
Herbert A. Giles
Herbert Carter
Herbert N. Casson
Herman Hesse
Hildegard G. Frey
Homer
Honore De Balzac
Horace B. Day
Horace Walpole
Horatio Alger Jr.
Howard Pyle
Howard R. Garis
Hugh Lofting
Hugh Walpole
Humphry Ward
Ian Maclaren
Inez Haynes Gillmore
Irving Bacheller
Isabel Cecilia Williams
Isabel Hornibrook
Israel Abrahams
Ivan Turgenev
J. G.Austin
J. Henri Fabre
J. M. Barrie
J. M. Walsh
J. Macdonald Oxley
J. R. Miller
J. S. Fletcher
J. S. Knowles
J. Storer Clouston
J. W. Duffield
Jack London
Jacob Abbott
James Allen
James Andrews
James Baldwin

James Branch Cabell
James DeMille
James Joyce
James Lane Allen
James Lane Allen
James Oliver Curwood
James Oppenheim
James Otis
James R. Driscoll
Jane Abbott
Jane Austen
Jane L. Stewart
Janet Aldridge
Jens Peter Jacobsen
Jerome K. Jerome
Jessie Graham Flower
John Buchan
John Burroughs
John Cournos
John F. Kennedy
John Gay
John Glasworthy
John Habberton
John Joy Bell
John Kendrick Bangs
John Milton
John Philip Sousa
John Taintor Foote
Jonas Lauritz Idemil Lie
Jonathan Swift
Joseph A. Altsheler
Joseph Carey
Joseph Conrad
Joseph E. Badger Jr
Joseph Hergesheimer
Joseph Jacobs
Jules Vernes
Julian Hawthrone
Julie A Lippmann
Justin Huntly McCarthy
Kakuzo Okakura
Karle Wilson Baker
Kate Chopin
Kenneth Grahame
Kenneth McGaffey
Kate Langley Bosher
Kate Langley Bosher
Katherine Cecil Thurston
Katherine Stokes
L. A. Abbot
L. T. Meade

L. Frank Baum
Latta Griswold
Laura Dent Crane
Laura Lee Hope
Laurence Housman
Lawrence Beasley
Leo Tolstoy
Leonid Andreyev
Lewis Carroll
Lewis Sperry Chafer
Lilian Bell
Lloyd Osbourne
Louis Hughes
Louis Joseph Vance
Louis Tracy
Louisa May Alcott
Lucy Fitch Perkins
Lucy Maud Montgomery
Luther Benson
Lydia Miller Middleton
Lyndon Orr
M. Corvus
M. H. Adams
Margaret E. Sangster
Margret Howth
Margaret Vandercook
Margaret W. Hungerford
Margret Penrose
Maria Edgeworth
Maria Thompson Daviess
Mariano Azuela
Marion Polk Angellotti
Mark Overton
Mark Twain
Mary Austin
Mary Catherine Crowley
Mary Cole
Mary Hastings Bradley
Mary Roberts Rinehart
Mary Rowlandson
M. Wollstonecraft Shelley
Maud Lindsay
Max Beerbohm
Myra Kelly
Nathaniel Hawthrone
Nicolo Machiavelli
O. F. Walton
Oscar Wilde
Owen Johnson
P.G. Wodehouse
Paul and Mabel Thorne

Paul G. Tomlinson
Paul Severing
Percy Brebner
Percy Keese Fitzhugh
Peter B. Kyne
Plato
Quincy Allen
R. Derby Holmes
R. L. Stevenson
R. S. Ball
Rabindranath Tagore
Rahul Alvares
Ralph Bonehill
Ralph Henry Barbour
Ralph Victor
Ralph Waldo Emmerson
Rene Descartes
Ray Cummings
Rex Beach
Rex E. Beach
Richard Harding Davis
Richard Jefferies
Richard Le Gallienne
Robert Barr
Robert Frost
Robert Gordon Anderson
Robert L. Drake
Robert Lansing
Robert Lynd
Robert Michael Ballantyne
Robert W. Chambers
Rosa Nouchette Carey
Rudyard Kipling
Saint Augustine
Samuel B. Allison
Samuel Hopkins Adams
Sarah Bernhardt
Sarah C. Hallowell
Selma Lagerlof
Sherwood Anderson
Sigmund Freud
Standish O'Grady
Stanley Weyman
Stella Benson
Stella M. Francis
Stephen Crane
Stewart Edward White
Stijn Streuvels
Swami Abhedananda
Swami Parmananda
T. S. Ackland

T. S. Arthur
The Princess Der Ling
Thomas A. Janvier
Thomas A Kempis
Thomas Anderton
Thomas Bailey Aldrich
Thomas Bulfinch
Thomas De Quincey
Thomas Dixon
Thomas H. Huxley
Thomas Hardy
Thomas More
Thornton W. Burgess
U. S. Grant
Upton Sinclair
Valentine Williams
Various Authors
Vaughan Kester
Victor Appleton
Victor G. Durham
Victoria Cross
Virginia Woolf
Wadsworth Camp
Walter Camp
Walter Scott
Washington Irving
Wilbur Lawton
Wilkie Collins
Willa Cather
Willard F. Baker
William Dean Howells
William le Queux
W. Makepeace Thackeray
William W. Walter
William Shakespeare
Winston Churchill
Yei Theodora Ozaki
Yogi Ramacharaka
Young E. Allison
Zane Grey